"YOUR EYES ARE LIKE STARS, HINTING OF UNLOCKED SECRETS AND BECKONING MY SOUL TO UKNOWN ADVENTURES."

Eleanor snatched her hands away. "Are you trying to seduce me, Mr. Weare?"

Egad, the chit was forthright. He smiled, liking more and more what he saw before him. "That's a rather unseemly question, Miss Carew."

"So is seduction, Mr. Weare. Unseemly."

There was something in the way this particular young lady looked at him that was boggling. He wanted her, perhaps more than any other, but not so soon, not now, and not regardless of the consequences. Looking at those golden-flecked eyes, those luscious red lips, and that enticing figure, he was lost. Miss Nora Carew, Litchfield decided, would be well worth the risk . . .

Lord Fortune's Prize

NANCY RICHARDS-AKERS

AVON BOOKS ◆ NEW YORK

LORD FORTUNE'S PRIZE is an original publication of Avon Books. This work has never before appeared in book form. This work is a novel. Any similarity to actual persons or events is purely coincidental.

AVON BOOKS
A division of
The Hearst Corporation
1350 Avenue of the Americas
New York, New York 10019

Copyright © 1993 by Nancy Richards-Akers
Published by arrangement with the author
Library of Congress Catalog Card Number: 92-97424
ISBN: 0-380-77191-8

First Avon Books Printing: June 1993

AVON TRADEMARK REG U.S. PAT OFF. AND IN OTHER COUNTRIES, MARCA REGISTRADA, HECHO EN U.S.A.

Printed in the U.S.A.

RA   10 9 8 7 6 5 4 3 2 1

For Juli Akers and Carolyn Akers Phillips,
May There Always Be Romance in Your Heart
and Success in All You Endeavor
and . . .
Of course, a lifetime of Merry Christmases.

One

 (decorative leaf ornament)

1814, Mayfair

"I F IT WAS LEGAL, I'd sell you!" the Earl of Mulgrave bellowed. "Never knew a daughter could be such a contrary creature. Positively unnatural. That's what you are."

The earl's voice echoed through the vaulted study of the Curzon Street town house, and despite a splitting headache owing to habitual overindulgence in smuggled French brandy, he managed to wave a menacing fist overhead. There was a slight wobble in his gait as he advanced toward the slender young woman seated by the hearth. Brandy sloshed from the snifter in his other hand to add yet another stain to the hand-knotted trio of dragons on the Axminster carpet, but nothing would deter him from delivering this ungrateful chit her rightful dressing-down.

"Sell you to the Gypsies. That's what I ought to do. Or to some Suleiman the Magnificent for his harem. I'm sure pashas pay handsomely for young Englishwomen. At least you've got good teeth."

Lady Eleanor Villiers sat statue-still, her back straight and her hands folded atop an open book resting upon her lap. Her steady gaze was focused upon the florid gentleman wearing a soiled waistcoat and sadly rumpled neckcloth. Not a single one of her delicate facial muscles revealed any trace of pain at the earl's harsh words. Eleanor had infinite practice at schooling her features into an unreadable expression, for she'd spent the past nineteen years hiding from her father the fact that his cruelty had ever hit its mark. Sitting a tad straighter, she smoothed the skirt of her sprigged muslin gown and waited for her father to finish his latest tirade.

"And don't look so demned superior," spat the earl, wishing that for once the wench might cower, that for once he might intimidate her as he had her mother. It was a hopeless ambition, for—he surmised with a ridiculous measure of vanity— Eleanor had inherited the Villiers strength of character, which was, in point of fact, a rather unbecoming trait for a female, and thus his pride gave way to disgust. "This time you're going to tow the line, Miss High and Mighty. Mark my words. I'll do it, y'know, rid myself of you once and for all. And you'll learn obedience, too, if I have to thrash it into you." He tossed the brandy snifter against the hearth, and the shattering of glass was accompanied by a sudden spurt of blue-gold flames.

Eleanor started. Her eyes widened, plain brown darkening to ink black orbs that appeared to be flecked with gold dust. A hand rose to her throat, and, fearing she had pushed him too far and was about to feel the backside of his hand, she inched as far as was possible into the depths of the winged chair. Yesterday the earl had struck his valet for no less than a missing waistcoat button, and Eleanor knew his violent temper made no exceptions for the weaker sex.

The earl emitted an ugly snicker. "I see you're not as dull as you'd like me to suppose. Got some reaction out of you at last." His cold eyes raked over her, and he frowned. When the earl looked at his daughter he didn't see exotic gold-flecked eyes or an enticing feminine figure and masses of wild curls the color of a moonless night; instead he saw the son he'd been denied and the unfortunate resemblance to his countess. Christ's nails, how he resented the pair of them, mother and daughter, and especially the woman he'd taken as wife. Lady Penelope had been a frail creature ill-suited to the necessities of childbirth and a poor excuse for a female in comparison to the company he kept at Madame Fournelle's on Lisle Street. The earl cursed, reached for another brandy snifter and poured a generous helping. Setting the decanter aside, he leveled an accusing finger at Eleanor. "You've been a gross disappointment from your first breath."

Unshed tears burned Eleanor's eyes, and, tilting her chin upward, she bit her lower lip. She had never let her father see her cry, not even at her mother's burial, and there was nothing he could say or do to change that. "I would be more than happy to return to the country, sir, if you like."

"If I *like*?" he sneered. "My dear, if you were so concerned with accommodating my wishes, you'd never have insulted m'pal Neddy Gatcombe with such an unrepentant refusal." The earl was referring to one of his gaming cronies who'd sought permission for Eleanor's hand in matrimony only to have been turned down. *Says she'll never submit to an arranged marriage*, a peeved Lord Gatcombe had reiterated the girl's refusal. Egad, an arranged marriage had been good enough for the girl's precious mother, hadn't it? Considering his daughter's uppity attitude, the earl's wrath reached new heights. "As for *your happiness*, I could care less. You've been in Town almost a month, but to what end? You're naught but a disappointment, though I shouldn't have expected otherwise. Much too

high and mighty for your own good. That's what
you are." He waved a dismissive hand. "The sight
of you makes me want to puke."

Eleanor didn't flinch. Over the years, he'd said
far worse, and in addition to developing the skills
to mask her emotions, Eleanor had learned to ease
the blow of his cruelty. As a child she'd found escape daydreaming of a tall stranger who would arrive at the gates of Mulgrave Manor upon a silver
steed. He would be as fair of face and heart as one
of King Richard's knights, and he'd be just bold
enough, just dangerous enough—this was the part
that always made her smile—to stand up to her father and set her free. Then she wouldn't have to
answer to anyone. She could make her own
choices and she would live her own life, not the
life someone else had decided for her. Then, certainly, she could go to sleep each night without
wondering about that whole great world—of people and wonders and adventures—which was beyond the bounds of Mulgrave Manor and which
she had been denied. It seemed a perfectly logical
ambition for a young lady whose lonely and iso-
lated childhood had been dictated by the will of a
selfish and bitter man, perfectly natural for a
young lady who'd watched her darling mama
wither away under that man's control.

Of course, the truth was there were no knights
crusading about the countryside. In fact, no one
ever visited Mulgrave Manor tucked away on the
lonely Berskire downs. Even the earl, who had
other estates in more favorable climes plus this elegant town house in Mayfair, made the trip to
Mulgrave Manor but twice a year. Besides, there
was nothing that could have convinced Eleanor to
leave Mulgrave Manor, if it had meant leaving her
mother behind.

Now, however, Lady Penelope was gone. Yet
Eleanor continued to struggle against her father's

control, and her future remained as unfulfilled as the gentle lady who lay at peace alongside her stillborn sons.

Lady Penelope's death hadn't been a great shock. This was not to say Lady Penelope wasn't deeply mourned, but she had been ill for a long time, and although a day never passed that Eleanor didn't yearn for her mother and the hours she spent at her bedside reading aloud from Miss Austen or Mrs. Radcliffe, Lady Penelope's death had been a relief.

From her earliest memories, Eleanor had been aware of her mother's suffering. That Lady Penelope no longer gasped for every breath was a blessing, but it was her emotional anguish that had been most painful for Eleanor to observe and from which she was most thankful her mother had been freed. That her arranged marriage to the Earl of Mulgrave and the almost annual loss of an unborn child caused Lady Penelope immense grief had been apparent to anyone who knew the gentle lady, yet to Eleanor another even more painful grief had been obvious. It had tormented Lady Penelope that the life into which she had brought her beautiful little daughter was one of virtual imprisonment, and Eleanor had been aware of that torment as surely as if it had been her own.

Eleanor knew how her mother had struggled to make her childhood as happy as was possible given the circumstances of a loveless marriage, a cruel and generally absent husband, and banishment at Mulgrave Manor. Since the moment of Eleanor's birth, mother and child had had no one save each other, and while their love knew no bounds, it wasn't the ideal situation for a little girl who needed friends and family and a father's love, nor was it adequate for a young mother who longed for the confidence of another lady and the attentions of a kind gentleman.

"When you give me the son and heir I desire, madam, then and only then shall I consider you wife. Until that time you will remain here with *that child*," the earl had said more than once when explaining why it was that Lady Penelope couldn't accompany him to London or another of his estates. As always every discussion with his wife concluded with a scornful reference to Eleanor.

Despite Lady Penelope's requests, mother and daughter never left Mulgrave Manor, and as *that child* had learned to conceal her emotions from her father, so, too, did she learn to keep them from her mother. It was an awful burden, but to Eleanor's credit her mother never suspected that Eleanor, who spent much of her time curled up on the library window seat with her nose buried in a book, wished that she might be anywhere else except at Mulgrave Manor and that she might be anyone other than herself. Lady Penelope never knew that her daughter's greatest wish was not to marry and have a family, but to be free to have a life of her own.

Eleanor had read about Venice and Cairo, Constaninople and Athens, and if the choice was hers, she thought it would be wonderful to visit those faraway places. It was her ambition to see the magnificent palaces and castles, to view the antiquities and great art, to attend the opera in Milan, see the ballet in St. Petersburg, and waltz in a splendid castle on the Rhine or perhaps in a villa above the Aegean Sea. While a husband and family might be nice for other young ladies, Eleanor knew such an arrangement was not for her. Independence was far preferable. It would guarantee that the absence of trust or loyalty or tenderness would not crush her as it had her mother. Eleanor would never allow herself to be at the whim of someone else.

While Lady Penelope's death had not been a shock, her father's appearance at the burial ceremony and the subsequent announcement of his plans for Eleanor's future had been horrifying in the extreme. Lady Penelope had often mentioned a small inheritance from her grandparents that had been set aside for her daughter, and, finding herself at the age of nineteen on her own, Eleanor believed she had the means to make her dreams come true. She decided to quit Mulgrave Manor and commence that independent life with a tour of the Continent. Of course, it was a wholly impractical notion since it neglected to take into account that a young lady couldn't travel without a companion, and it was all the more impractical since her father controlled that inheritance. Less than four hours after Lady Penelope's internment, the earl announced that he intended to use it for Eleanor's dowry.

"We need to make you as attractive as possible," the earl had declared between gulps of brandy. According to her father, they were leaving Mulgrave Manor for London at first light. Eleanor was to move into the town house on Curzon Street and have a full Season with all the trappings necessary to make quick work of snaring a husband. "I intend to have you dispatched to the altar before summer's spent."

"I've no desire to be paraded on the marriage mart like a prime piece of cattle," Eleanor had protested. "I fear, sir, a Season does not appeal to me in the least."

This interview in the library at Mulgrave Manor had been the first time that father and daughter had exchanged more than two or three sentences. Verily, the earl had never been alone in a room with Eleanor, no less sought to know anything about her interests or talents, and, truth to tell, would probably have passed by his only offspring on the street as if she were a stranger. Neither father nor daughter had been prepared for the ensuing pyrotechnics.

"Never heard the likes of it," he had rejoined, his anger momentarily tempered by astonishment. "All proper young ladies aspire to a Season and marriage. Ain't queer in the attic, are you? Only thing worse than a daughter would be a beetle-headed daughter."

"No, sir. Your daughter is no idiot." In the hopes it might impress him, Eleanor had added as an afterthought, "I'm quite well read, in fact."

"Well read, you say." The earl's tone had been scornful. "I don't recall hiring a tutor for you."

"You didn't, sir. My mother taught me what she knew, and when she was too ill to continue, I taught myself."

"Yes. Yes. Well, I wager you're quite proud of your needlepoint skills," he had said in the most annoyingly condescending manner.

"No, sir, my needlepoint skills are mediocre. I am, however, quite proud of my translation of Homer." Eleanor was boastful of this accomplishment, for reading books and gaining knowledge were the only truly independent choices she'd made for herself.

He'd gasped as if he were the victim of a sudden apoplectic attack. "Egad, you'll keep such freakish things to yourself. Do you hear me? And what, pray tell, do you intend, if not a Season and a stroll down the aisle at St. Paul's? I won't countenance a bluestocking any more than an idiot, y'know."

"I've never considered myself a bluestocking, but I do confess to a profound curiosity about the world at large, and I had thought that perhaps in lieu of a Season a Continental tour would be nice," she had confided.

"*Nice!*" The earl's complexion had been a livid carmine. "How dare you mock me!"

"I did not intend any disrespect."

"Did you not? To suggest to a man with no heir that you might enjoy a privilege to which sons, not daughters, are entitled? Indeed, you mock me."

Eleanor had owned genuine shame that he might think her so thoughtless. "You must understand, sir, that I've little experience in the world."

"And thus you blame me for such wanton stupidity."

"No, sir, I merely ask for your patience."

"Hah, patience! Next you'll be asking for my indulgence," he had taunted. "Well, it won't happen. I'm not a patient man. I don't like waiting, and right now I want you to instruct the housekeeper to pack your bags. You're to be ready to leave this place in the morning." He had glanced about the library as if seeing his surroundings for the first time. The girl had told him this was her favorite room in the Queen Anne manor house, but he didn't like it. Libraries were supposed to be dark quiet places, not shining with sunlight spilling across a stenciled floor covering, or overflowing with flowers atop every bit of space and bright chintz cushions piled on overstuffed chairs and cozy window seats. A library was a man's domain, but this room bore the mark of his countess and that child. His scowl had deepened. He'd never been fond of Mulgrave Manor, and he wanted to quit the premises as soon as possible. "I'm taking you to London. You'll comply, and, if needs be, by force."

"Why would you force me?" Eleanor had asked. "I don't understand. Why do you care? Why not leave me to my own devices? I won't be any bother, I promise. What possible satisfaction can there be for you? Certainly you don't imagine to make amends for nineteen years of neglect."

"You're quite right." He had emitted an ugly snort of laughter. "This has nothing to do with paternal affection or duty, or assuaging some imagined guilt. Let me explain something, m'dear. First, as far as I'm concerned a daughter's a commodity. Nothing more. Second, I'm a man who often needs a favor or two, and I know a number of gentlemen who would gladly go into debt to me in exchange for a young bride. It's a simple enough equation. Your taking a walk up the aisle with the right fellow would mean money in the bank, so to speak, and I can't afford to overlook that sort of insurance."

Eleanor had been outraged, and she retorted without thinking. "Even if I agree to accompany you to Town, you can't make me wed against my will, nor be pleasant, nor go along with any of your plans for that matter."

The earl's fist had crashed down on the nearest surface, causing a decorative semi-circle of Chelsea shepherdesses to fall to the floor where they broke, jagged bits of glazed porcelain scattering across the carpet. Lady Penelope had been immeasurably fond of those figurines, treasuring them for the memories associated with them. How often she had related to Eleanor the various occasions upon which she had acquired them. The shepherdess in pink had been a birthday gift, the one in pale blue had been stuffed in a woolen stocking one Christmas, and the one in bright yellow herding a flock of lambs had been a New Year's present from her father, Sir Christopher Verney.

Stifling a cry of dismay, Eleanor had knelt to gather up the severed bonnets, broken crooks, and shattered lambs. A fierce anger rose within her, and, pausing to look up at her father, she had revealed her unguarded feelings. Loathing and accusation had been etched upon her features. Her dark eyes had blazed with golden fury. High color had touched her cheeks.

The earl was familiar with such looks. He'd seen them on his lady wife's face in the early months of their marriage before he'd managed to smother her spirit. He didn't like seeing them now any more than he did then. What was wrong with the chit? Didn't she understand? No one crossed the Earl of Mulgrave without paying the consequences.

"Damn you!" he had growled as he kicked the nearest bit of shepherdess, shattering it into three smaller, unrecognizable pieces.

To Eleanor, it was almost as if the earl had struck her mother. The color had faded from her cheeks, and her eyes had paled to an unremarkable brown as she had disguised the direction of her thoughts. She had a choice here, albeit not the brightest, but it was nonetheless a choice. She could submit to her father and go along with his every scheme, or she could decide to do whatever was necessary to attain the independence she coveted.

"Fine, sir. I yield to your wishes and shall be ready to travel at first light," she'd agreed in a most docile fashion, all the while thinking that her father didn't have to know she had other plans. Going to London as he demanded would be nothing more than a means to an end. Her end. It was the most expeditious way to leave Mulgrave Manor, and once in London, when the time was right, Eleanor would slip away to start a life of her own.

She had promised herself never to be at the whim of someone else, and she would be true to that promise. She would make her own choices about her future. Of course, she'd probably never get to see those faraway places, but that was all right. Anything would be better than what her father intended for her. She didn't care if she had to work. Perhaps she could obtain employment as a companion or a parlor maid. Anything would be preferable to submitting to a loveless union and finding herself trapped as her mother had been.

Two

<RESIDENCE AT HER> father's Curzon Street town house was not the trial Eleanor had imagined. To her delight, living beneath his roof afforded her a theretofore unknown freedom. Accounts were opened in her name with the fashionable modiste Madame Cruesset and at several shops in the Burlington Arcade, where Eleanor enjoyed browsing and purchasing whatever trinket or bonnet caught her eye. The choices were endless. From Mr. Tilbury's on Mount Street, a driver and landau were hired and put at her disposal, and every afternoon at the fashionable hour she lined up with the crush of vehicles to make the circuit through Hyde Park. She could make her own decisions about what to do and where to go, and, for the time being, the thought of flight from her father's household seemed foolish when there was so much to explore in the bustling metropolis.

The earl never rose until dusk, leaving Eleanor to her own devices. His only demand was that she be appropriately dressed and ready to attend whatever social function was on the calendar each evening. The earl's sordid reputation notwithstanding, the matrons of Mayfair remembered Lady Penelope Verney, a girl whose lineage was impeccable and whose sensibilities and beauty had been most remarkable, and out of respect for the departed gentle lady, they invited Eleanor into their saloons and ballrooms. There was an endless round of musicales and card parties, soirees, levees, and balls, and each night, the earl remained sober long enough to escort Eleanor to the particular affair and introduce her to their host and hostess. After an hour or so, he would slip away, leaving Eleanor in the care of some sympathetic dowager, usually his eccentric neighbor, the Dowager Duchess of Exeter. Eleanor wasn't sure where he went. Her new friend, the dowager duchess's niece, Lady Eglantine Paget, told Eleanor that she had overheard something about *hedonistic pursuits* and a woman who staged cockfights in her saloon on Lisle Street. It sounded revolting and low and just what she expected of her father. Eleanor did not care to know the details. All that mattered was that her days were hers to do with as she pleased. Eleanor was in charge, she could make her own decisions, and it was no surprise that she liked it very much.

The British Museum quickly became her favorite haunt. There she could glimpse a sampling of the wonders that had filled the library books at Mulgrave Manor. There were gods made of gold from Greece and Rome and Egypt, and vessels of agate and jaspis from the coffers of ancient kings. From the pyramids along the Nile there were mummies, a giant black sarcophagus, and a pair of colossal lions. There were myriad natural curiosities as well. Eleanor marveled at butterflies the size of a gentleman's hand and the color of a blazing sunset, and she regarded with a mixture of fascination and revulsion the spiders as big as geese, the crocodiles, hippopotamuses, and sharks.

Sometimes Lady Eglantine would accompany her, but more often than not Eleanor went alone. It was her practice to arrive at Montague House in

Bloomsbury when the doors first opened to admit the public and stay until closing, often being the final visitor to exit the massive temple-like front doors.

On one such particular day, a storm had blown up the Thames, and Eleanor, unprepared for inclement weather, had found herself facing Great Russell Street without a parasol and barely able to discern the outline of her hired landau waiting outside the gate. She waved to Tom Pease, the coachman, to come with an oilcloth, but he didn't see her. It was late. She was due at Exeter House within the hour. The Dowager Duchess of Exeter was hostessing a small dinner dance, and Eleanor and Lady Eglantine had planned on getting ready for the party together. Eleanor called out to the coachman, but he didn't hear her. She needed to be on her way home, and, having decided to make a dash for the landau, she left the safety of the portico just as a sudden gust of wind swept her off her feet.

It was almost like flying, so strong was the wind that she was quite cosseted by its power, and welcome memories of Mulgrave Manor surfaced upon her mind's eye. As a child she'd often slipped outside to dance in the courtyard beneath a cloudburst. Of course, Lady Penelope had reprimanded Eleanor, warning of the dangers of lightning and urging her daughter to come inside and sit upon the library window seat, if she desired to view nature's tempest.

Eleanor was fascinated by the rain and wind. They awakened her senses, making her feel free. She could imagine she was standing on the threshold of adventure, and even this unexpected tumble was thrilling. It was curious to float as if she were nothing more than a stray leaf without bonds to anyone or anything, and for the briefest moment, Eleanor wasn't aware of the sting of the needle-sharp raindrops, nor did she hear the crash of thunder overhead.

In a matter of seconds, however, this most peculiar interlude came to a halt as she hurled with full force against something exceedingly hard. Oddly enough she remained upright, and although the breath was knocked from her, Eleanor hadn't lost her wits. She knew right away that she had collided with a man, who proceeded in the next instant to sweep her off her feet and carry her back up the stairs. She knew, too, that she had been saved from certain injury, and, caring not a wit for propriety, Eleanor wrapped her arms about her rescuer's neck and rested against this chest. There was shelter from the storm against his solid form, and she leaned as close to that comfort as she could.

In several strides, they reached the portico, and, thus out of the downpour, the gentleman set Eleanor upon her feet. Any other young lady would have submitted to a fit of the vapors at the horror of her narrow escape and such intimate closeness to a stranger of the male gender, but not Lady Eleanor. Quite to the contrary, she was reluctant to step away from him. Having never been embraced by anyone other than her frail mother, Eleanor found this man's strength to be at once as intriguing as it was comforting. He was a stranger, perhaps not even a gentleman, yet she didn't want this moment to pass. Just as she reveled in the experience of being lighter than air, just as she relished the sensations of a cool rain and savored the sights and sounds of the bustling metropolis, Eleanor wished to satisfy her curiosity about this man, and she lingered beside him with a growing awareness of the mingling aromas of leather and lime, not an altogether unpleasant combination of odors. It was giddy and wanton to consider whether or not a man smelled nice. But she couldn't pretend otherwise, nor deny that it was true, and wondering what this gentleman of lime and leather might look like, she tilted her head back.

Her first impression was of height. He was a tall man, so tall she could scarcely make out his features. And broad, so broad that his solid form blocked out the storm. She had a view of a well-defined jaw, the end of an aristocratic nose, and the inside brim of a gentleman's beaver hat that was dripping water on her. Two raindrops landed in the middle of her forehead. They tickled, and without much success Eleanor endeavored to suppress a giggle.

"I can't see you, you know," was her ingenuous declaration, her words mingling with laughter. "You're far too tall, sir. It's rather like being rescued by a greatcoat."

The gentleman didn't say anything. Instead, he backed down the stairs until he stood before Eleanor, and when they faced eye-to-eye, he cocked his head to one side and offered her a devil-may-care grin that seemed to say, *Go ahead and take your best look. I trust I'll pass muster.*

Which is exactly what Eleanor did without the least bit of shame or prudery. There was nothing reticent about Eleanor, and after a few seconds, she began to smile, for the face that was revealed to her was quite handsome. Actually, she had to admit, handsome was not sufficient to describe him. He was beautiful. Intriguingly, dramatically perfect for a man with a lean sculptured face and the sort of skin that brings to mind a flushed complexion after one has come inside from a rousing gallop across a sun-drenched meadow. Beneath the faint shadow of a beard, the strong lines of his jaw and chiseled cheekbones were elegant. Eleanor's tall rescuer possessed that variety of refined masculine features that when combined with

fair hair and blue eyes never failed to fascinate the
weaker sex, and the innocent Eleanor was no exception. The gentleman's hair, thick and straight
and the color of ripe wheat, reminded her of the
choir boys at Westminster Abbey, while the moon-
shaped scar below his right eye was positively
roguish. Again, she suppressed a giggle at the notion that he was actually a devil in disguise, but
when she looked into his eyes, deep and blue and
pure, that impression vanished. For in those pure
blue eyes Eleanor imagined she saw the knight of
her childhood fantasy.

Standing no more than four or five inches away
from her, he was as fair of face as she had always
imagined, and her heart somersaulted. Eleanor
needed to know if he was real, and there was only
one way to find out.

Her hand rose to touch his face, and, trailing up
the line of his jaw, her fingers began to tremble
with discovery. The skin was warm and a little
rough. It was hard, too, not soft and pliant like her
own flesh, and her breath caught at the unexpected weakness this caused her. Curious to know
more, her hand paused below his right eye, and
she allowed one fingertip to touch the dimpled
edge of that half-moon scar.

His response was immediate, and Eleanor
pulled back her hand and her gaze widened as a
harsh sound seemed to be torn from deep within
him.

Wondering what this sudden outburst might
mean, Eleanor glanced from the scar into his eyes,
and what she saw within those blue depths made
her even weaker. There was fire in his regard. It
was smoldering. She'd read about such looks in
Minerva novels, heard other girls whisper in the
ladies' cloakroom at Almack's about heated gazes,
but until this moment she had never understood
what they meant. Now she knew, and they were

right. It was at once dangerous and thrilling, and Eleanor's face grew warm.

The tall gentleman smiled as if he knew precisely what she was thinking. It was a frightfully discomposing smile, far too worldly and far too confident. Her knight was supposed to liberate her, not confuse her like this. Eleanor took several quick steps away from him. Her regard, however, did not waver from those blue eyes, and she held her breath as his gaze moved toward her lips. Lord, this was unsettling, and Eleanor swallowed hard, feeling as if she ought to run for safety, but she was paralyzed as a cornered rabbit.

What happened next came quickly. In one smooth stride, the gentleman closed the small distance that Eleanor had made between them, and before she could react, he enfolded her in his arms and lowered his lips to lightly brush hers in a gentle kiss. He nibbled at the corners of her mouth, making Eleanor breathless as the pressure of his lips became more insistent. His mouth quickened to move more swiftly over hers, his fingers caressing her face in tantalizing counterpoint to his lips, which were so tender, yet demanding.

It was glorious. Divine. Spellbinding. Eleanor's knees trembled, and her head spun in dizzying circles. *I must have knocked myself on the cobblestones. Perhaps I'm dead, and this is heaven.* She'd never given much thought to kisses, but she knew in this instant that she liked them and all the accompanying sensations very much.

"My lady, pardon me for interfering." A familiar voice intruded on this exquisite moment.

The gentleman stopped kissing Eleanor, his lips left hers, and when he raised his head a small cry of dismay escaped her. She couldn't help it. That wasn't all there could be, was it? Why did it have to end like that? Suddenly, she was aware of the painful beating of her heart and a throat so dry she could scarcely swallow. As if she had fallen victim to some heathen spell, Eleanor was neither awake nor asleep. She blinked her eyes several times and shook her head.

The world around her seemed as if she were peering through the wrong end of a telescope. Tom Pease, the hired coachman, was holding out an oilcloth, but he appeared to be standing leagues away at some exceedingly far and unreachable distance. Slowly, she looked back to the blue-eyed gentleman, who was in perfect focus. He was studying her, those clear blue eyes filled with such intensity that Eleanor was certain he'd glimpsed into her soul and knew her every innermost secret. He even knew she liked to be kissed. Eleanor blushed.

"My lady, are you all right? This gentleman hasn't been bothering you, has he?" Tom Pease was insistent.

This time, the coachman's voice broke whatever spell enthralled Eleanor, and she started as if waking, but it hadn't been a dream. That kiss had been real, and those alien, yet shockingly pleasurable sensations had been real, perhaps the most real thing of her entire young and sheltered life.

"Thank you, sir," she whispered to the gentleman. There was a throaty quality in her voice that sounded not at all like herself. She had to leave.

"I haven't rescued many ladies, but it was a pleasure," the gentleman whispered in reply. His voice rumbled as deep as the thunder, yet fell upon her as softly as a caress. Eleanor trembled anew.

The coachman positioned the oilcloth in the air like a tent and waited for his mistress.

"You'll be safe now," the gentleman told Eleanor, yet he held her still.

Overhead, there was a deafening volley of thunder.

"We must hurry, my lady," this entreaty came from Tom Pease.

Eleanor allowed the coachman to guide her down the slick marble stairs. Rain pelted the oilcloth and a gust of wind tugged at her skirt, but Eleanor was preoccupied. How could any gentleman produce such a disarming effect upon her? It was highly irregular. Perhaps it was nothing more than the storm. After all, she knew nothing about kisses and whether or not they all ended like that. In the next instant, she couldn't stop herself from wondering if she would ever see this particular gentleman again. Probably not, in which case she'd never know any more about kisses than she already did, nor why it was that her heart had quickened and her knees had weakened.

Halfway to the landau, something compelled Eleanor to look over her shoulder for one last glance at the tall man with the fair face and clear blue eyes. Perhaps there was such a thing as fate or precognition. Her mother had believed in them. *You must never fight fate,* Lady Penelope had often told Eleanor. *There's no such thing as coincidence.*

Maybe her mother had been right and Eleanor's dream of the knight hadn't been a fantasy, but a vision, and the gentleman's arrival at this precise time and place was a sign that she would soon leave her father's home. After all, the gentleman had rescued her, and although it hadn't been at all like her dreams, that didn't matter. Eleanor's countenance brightened, and as the sun peeped out from behind a cloud, casting silver light across the wet cobbles, she began to laugh.

Three

ADDISON WEARE, THE Right Honorable Earl of
Litchfield, hadn't slept in three nights. At
least not in his own bed, and the thrashing rain
felt good as he made his way down Great Russell
Street in Bloomsbury. The spring storm was re-
freshing and exhilarating. Of course, it wasn't the
same sort of thrill as racing one's curricle on a narrow country lane or facing the champion pugilist
Tom Cribb with bare fists. Nonetheless it was
rousing.

A long volley of thunder rumbled from the dark
clouds, and a vivid image of pirate ships exchang-
ing cannon fire filled his mind's eye. He was
standing at the ship's prow. His gleaming sword
was drawn, the wind was screaming about him,
and he knew he was willing to fight to the death.

Such a fantasy would have generated a vast
amount of ridicule in Litchfield's jaded set. The
earl didn't mix in Polite Society, his companions in
the pursuit of pleasure being drawn from the
ranks of London's more notorious wastrels. Scoun-
drels one and all, they were gentlemen who lived
for the moment at hand, and, indeed, they would
have mocked his indulgence in such a schoolboy
fancy. But no one needed to know how Litchfield
had longed for such adventures as a lad. No one

needed to know that the Twelfth Earl of Litchfield
had not always been as reckless and indifferent as
Society believed him to be; that once upon a time,
after his parents had died and before he had become known as Lord Fortune, the Earl of
Litchfield had been a lonely frightened lad whose
only playmates had been from the realm of make-
believe.

Perhaps it was Montague House, maybe the
rain, that caused these distempered thoughts to
flash through his brain. It had been a long time,
six or seven years, since he'd thought of that pirate
ship, since he'd given more than the briefest consideration to old memories, and of course, in all
that time, he'd never breathed a word of it to anyone. No one of his current circle of associates
would have understood the importance of that
daydream, and besides, it wasn't important anymore. It was part of a past that was very different
and very distant from the man he had become.

Such a boyhood fantasy was of little value. In
fact, the most important thing in Lord Litchfield's
life on this particular afternoon was Lady Maria
Putney. Specifically, the question of how to sever
his relationship with the cloying lady had been on
his mind since daybreak when she had threatened
to throw herself off Blackfriars Bridge if he didn't
marry her before the Season's end.

Litchfield loathed emotional scenes, perhaps because he himself seldom revealed his sensibilities.
They were such a nuisance. For where there were
emotions, trouble of one sort or another wasn't far
behind. One could deal quite nicely without them,
he'd discovered. They were rather repulsive, in
point of fact. After this morning, for example, he'd
never be able to remember Lady Maria's soft
blonde hair and welcoming body, instead he
would recall her bloated, tear-streaked face and
deafening fishwife's screech. In hindsight, he

shouldn't have gotten involved with Maria
Putney, who wasn't really a lady despite her marriage to the deceased Lord Frederick. She was the
daughter of a cit, and her manners in the heat of
passion were most revealing. He needed to disen-
cumber himself of the creature, and how to do it
without enduring another nasty scene presented a
most vexing situation.

The storm, therefore, was a relief. Litchfield
tossed back his head and closed his eyes to experience the sensation of sharp raindrops against his
face. After a time, he opened his eyes, and that
was when he noticed a slender female standing
beneath the portico of Montague House. His first
reaction was distinctly predatory, a normal reaction for Lord Fortune, who was always ready and
willing to add another female to his list of con-
quests. Was the young lady chaperoned? he wondered. And, if she was pleasing to the eye, might
she be interested in passing the storm in his company?

She appeared to be a young lady of breeding
and means, dressed as she was in a stylish bishop's blue walking outfit complete with matching
bonnet, and it surprised him when she dashed
from beneath the protection of the portico and
headlong into the storm. She would be drenched
in no time, and there was no doubt she would in-
cur the wrath of a chaperon or indignant mama
upon returning home, for proper young ladies did
not expose themselves to the elements. As the
thunder roared overhead, he fancied she was a
kindred spirit, and he imagined her standing beside him at the prow of that pirate ship preparing
to go ashore to explore some faraway tropical isle.

Devil a bit, his mind was idling down the most
ludicrous paths. He was destined for Bedlam. No
doubt about it. Perhaps it wouldn't hurt to slow
his pace, and once rid of Lady Maria he could rus-

ticate at his Hampshire estate for a few weeks. He
chuckled at the rumors such uncharacteristic behavior would elicit, but this self-absorbed amusement died when he saw the young lady in
bishop's blue lose her footing and career through
the air. Although rescue was foremost on his mind
as he headed toward her, there was no denying
that he liked the notion of having a young lady
land in his arms. It was Providence that had
brought him here this afternoon just as he was de-
termining the most expeditious way to divest himself of Lady Maria. Thanks to good fortune, it
appeared he wouldn't want for company.

In four strides, he positioned himself in such a
way that he stopped her body with his own, his
arms wrapping about her shoulders and holding
her close to prevent the pair of them from tumbling the remainder of the distance to the side-
walk. She was light as a feather, and he swept her
into his arms and bounded up the staircase to the
shelter. Keeping a firm hold about her waist, he
put her on her feet and braced himself for an on-
slaught of female histrionics. He fully expected her
to flutter her eyelashes, cry out for recuperative
salts and faint into a Drury Lane swoon. Instead,
she surprised him with a warble of sweet laughter
that seemed to him as clear and bright as church
bells on a crisp autumn morning.

This uncommon female further surprised
Litchfield with an outburst of speech.

"I can't see you, you know. You're far too tall,"
she declared in a voice that revealed curiosity as
well as a touch of annoyance. Again, she laughed.
"It's rather like being rescued by a greatcoat."

She was charming. Intriguing. And wanting to
know what this unique young lady looked like,
Litchfield moved down two steps to stand eye-to-
eye and study her with bold regard. What he saw
quite pleased him, for she was exquisite far be-

yond anything he could have imagined. A riot of
raven curls framed a heart-shaped face with full
ruby lips and eyes that were flecked with gold.
She reminded him of a Gypsy, almost too exotic
for a lady, and his mind flew back to when they'd
collided. The memory of soft breasts and a slender
waist roused him, and in that instant, he considered her with one purpose in mind. Seduction and
bedding. The one purpose for which he believed
all women had been created.

The Earl of Litchfield liked women. He liked
them a great deal ever since he'd been fifteen and
the upstairs maid had invited him into the linen
closet. He liked all women. Tall or short, thin or
full-figured, fair or dark, it made no matter. He
had no specific preferences, for in each woman he
found something distinctive to desire, and to his
delight, women had always liked him. In his
twenty-eight years, he'd had mistresses too nu-
merous to detail and had enjoyed countless en-
counters with females of all classes. If he liked
what he saw, he had it. Ever since the upstairs
maid, it had always been that easy, and right now
Lord Litchfield liked what he saw.

He was casting about for the next thing to say
when she surprised him once more by reaching up
to trail the backside of her hand along his jaw.
Stunned, he swallowed hard, and again, he studied her expression, noting the absence of coquetry
in her demeanor. Her touch was not flirtatious. It
was tentative, and he watched in delight as her
eyes widened with discovery. He recognized the
signs. She'd never touched a man; more importantly, no man had ever touched her, and fully expecting her to pull away from him, he was
amazed when her hand stopped and she allowed
one fingertip to touch the edge of his scar.

It wasn't a caress in an amorous sense, but the
tenderness of this touch affected him nonetheless.

Desire coiled within him. He groaned. Their gazes locked, and he saw fear flicker in her eyes, for he knew his features were alive with a wanting he could no longer control.

This time, she did back away from him, but it was pointless.

In a quick series of movements, Litchfield pulled her to him and put his mouth over hers. She smelled of lavender and moist clean hair. She was sweet and pure and he wanted her, and, having substituted physical intimacy for more meaningful attachments for far too long, he kissed her with all the desperation and hunger of a man so lost he doesn't know what he needs to survive.

A voice intruded. "My lady."

Litchfield looked up to see a coachman standing nearby, then he glanced back to the young woman in his arms and recognized the sleepy-lidded veil of first passion upon those gold-flecked eyes. A delicate flush fanned across her forehead and cheeks, and he ran a long careless finger down one warm feather-soft cheek.

The coachman repeated himself, and the young woman whispered to Litchfield, "Thank you, sir."

"I haven't rescued many ladies, but it was a pleasure," he replied, regretting right away this suggestive choice of words. Somehow they didn't seem as clever as he'd thought. The young lady, however, did not seem to comprehend the direction of his remark. "You'll be safe now," he added in a gentle tone, knowing that it was from him and not the storm from which she needed protection.

The coachman escorted her down the stairs. Litchfield frowned. It was entirely out of character to let such a beauty escape without even asking her name. Ah, well, he gave a shrug. Perhaps it hadn't been meant to be.

Four

E LEANOR LOST NO time in relating the details of
her rescue on the steps of Montague House
to Lady Eglantine, who heaved a melodramatic
sigh upon learning that a mysterious gentleman
had swept her friend off her feet and into his
arms.

"An encounter in the rain—oh, Eleanor. A rescue, no less, by a stranger. Why, it's quite *the most
perfectly* romantic thing *I can imagine*," Lady Eglantine pronounced, which was a significant statement since she was considered a thoroughly
incurable romantic. What other young lady fell in
and out of love as easily as changing satin slippers? Already this Season, there had been a spate
of gentlemen in uniforms. Captain Andrews of the
King's Dragoons, Major Lord Etherington of the
Life Guards, and Colonel Ferguson of the Scots
Greys—each of them an irresistibly dashing speci-
men in full military regalia. Lady Eglantine believed in love at first sight, and she sighed again.
"Oh, to be swept off my feet by a tall handsome
stranger. I'm pea-green with envy, you know. It
doesn't seem in the least bit fair. For all those
times I've traipsed off with you to Montague
House and been bored to tears, one would think
that *something* would happen to me. Just a tiny re-

ward. My life's such a bore. Nothing *ever* happens
to me."

Eleanor ignored this impassioned outburst. As
much as she adored Eglantine, her friend owned
two lamentable habits. A penchant for dramatic
overstatement, and the tendency to fret that every-
body else had a life more exciting than hers. There
was a much more pressing matter to address than
Eglantine's imagined social hardships. Eleanor
looked her straight in the eye. "You must promise
not to tell anyone about what I've just told you,
Eglantine. You will promise, won't you?"

"Oh, you mustn't harass yourself," came Eglantine's careless reply.

The young ladies were in Eglantine's bedchamber at Exeter House putting the final touches on
their toilette before going downstairs to join the
dowager duchess's guests. It was to be a small
group, mostly young people for dancing and a
buffet supper. Eleanor and Eglantine had been
particularly looking forward to the evening because Eglantine's scapegrace brother, the Viscount
Dalsany, and his new wife would be there. Of
course, Eglantine already knew Lady Priscilla Fox-
Strangways. They'd grown up together in Dorset,
and she couldn't wait to introduce the pair to
Eleanor, who was curious to meet Dalsany and his
bride, who'd defied her family to marry a gentleman with the reputation of a rakehell.

"You must promise," Eleanor repeated.

"All right, I shan't breathe a word of it to anyone, excepting, of course, Great-Aunt Margaret.
That's all right, isn't it? She'll be as thrilled as I
am, you know."

Lady Eglantine's great-aunt Margaret was the
Dowager Duchess of Exeter, a veritable social icon
far better known for her eccentricities than the
customary high-stickling ways of the Upper Ten
Thousand. Last Season, she had shocked the *ton*

when she opened Exeter House after a twelve-year
retreat from Society to hostess a gala in aid of Viscount Dalsany's desperate search for a suitable
wife. This Season, the dowager duchess was spon-
soring her great-niece, and Exeter House had already been the site of several elegant fetes,
although the guest lists had been restricted, for the
dowager duchess did not countenance chatter-
boxes, cakes, fribbles, or tattlemongers. There was
nothing more unbecoming than a young lady
taken to batting her eyelashes and lisping like an
infant. Nothing more tiresome than a fop whose
self-esteem hinged on cataloguing the shortcomings of others. Hypocrites one and all, the dowager duchess had dubbed them, and she had
advised Lady Eglantine not to judge a gentleman
by appearance or by Society's verdict. Neither
were reliable barometers.

"If you wish to marry and be happy, look
among the rakes, m'dear gel," the dowager duchess had been heard to say on more than one occasion. She had wed one of the previous century's
most notorious rakehells, and, unlike most of her
contemporaries, the Duchess of Exeter had found
matrimony a highly satisfactory arrangement.
"There's nothing better than a rake," was her
grace's credo. She was a wise and kindhearted
lady, who was determined that her great-niece
find happiness. Being a diamond of the first water
was not important, and she was pleased that Eglantine needed no convincing when it came to
marrying for anything less than true love.

It pleased her, too, when the Earl of Mulgrave
brought his daughter to Town. Exeter House was
around the corner from the earl's Curzon Street
residence, and the dowager duchess, finding that
she quite enjoyed the role she had assumed vis-á-
vis her great-niece, took Eleanor under her wing
as well. Being of a like age and having no other

acquaintances in Town, the girls also liked this arrangment, although they often suspected that were anyone to realize the sorts of things the dowager duchess was whispering in their ears they would have been whisked off to the nearest convent for a serious regimen of reeducation, repentance, and reform.

"Of course you may tell your great-aunt, but no one else. Not even your abigail," Eleanor emphasized. Eglantine was inordinately fond of gossip when there was the hint of romance, and Eleanor knew only too well how rumors filtered below stairs and between the servants' quarters to fly through London's fashionable West End. If Eglantine's abigail knew, then it would be no time before her father's valet knew that his daughter had been in the arms of a strange man. "There's no telling what my father would do if he found out. He believes I'm trying to sabotage his efforts to find me a husband, and he threatened me again last night, you know."

"Another pasha?" Eglantine asked, opening her jewelry box to inspect the contents.

"No." Eleanor went to stand before the pier glass and adjust the bodice of her new gown. "This time it was a recuperative voyage to Botany Bay, if he could find the judge to arrange it."

"Oh, Eleanor, that's a truly horrid thing to say to one's own child. It's inexcusable." Lady Eglantine, who had been raised in a loving household, looked at her friend in sympathy. Even her brother, despite his shortcomings, had never been cast out from the fold. "I'm so sorry you should have to deal with such unpleasantries."

"You mustn't be sorry on my account. I'm not in the least, nor do I take his threats seriously. At least not regarding pashas or Botany Bay. As for an arranged marriage, that's another matter, for now that I've turned down Lord Gatcombe, I fear my father's trying to hatch up some other candidate." Eleanor essayed an off-hand tone as she made a quarter-turn in front of the mirror. Madame Cruesset had been right. The dark green satin gown complemented her black hair quite nicely, and Eleanor was glad she'd allowed the modiste to talk her into the purchase. She patted her hair, arranged *á la* Venus, and pinched her cheeks to give them a bit more color, then glanced over her shoulder at Eglantine. "If only my father would grant me the right to decide upon the direction of my future, I would soon be gone from his household. I want nothing from him save my independence, but I fear that's impossible."

"Which is precisely why you must find your tall, blue-eyed gentleman, make him fall madly in love with you, and elope to Gretna Green," Eglantine asserted, as if such a sequence of events might be accomplished before afternoon tea. She was sorting through a velvet-lined tray of brooches, and her hand flittered back and forth between an opal brooch from Captain Andrews and one from Colonel Ferguson of amethysts sparkling on a sprig of silver heather. Earlier in the Season, word had circulated that the lovely Lady Eglantine had a fondness for brooches, and now there were four other glittering creations upon the tray. The dowager duchess had scolded her great-niece for accepting those lavish gifts, but they were such pretty baubles Eglantine couldn't bear to part with them. She decided to wear them all, pinning them in random fashion about the skirt of her gown. The display of sparkling brooches was quite perfect, lending the appearance of stars in the sky against the royal blue fabric. Done with pinning, she continued her discourse with Eleanor as if she hadn't lost a beat.

"And if you don't favor the notion of marriage over the anvil to this gentleman, there's always a special license. I've a relative who's a representative of the archbishop, and if he helped my brother, I'm sure he'd help a friend of mine. Now, do tell me, how does this look?" She gave a twirl to display the brooches.

"Fine," replied Eleanor. "But can't we stick to the subject?"

"Oh, yes. Of course. Marriage to your blue-eyed gentleman. Special license or Gretna Green. Now which shall it be? I rather prefer special license myself. Then, at least, you can wed with some of the requisite trappings. I'd hate to sacrifice a walk down the aisle, all those flowers, and all that fabulous organ music even for true love."

"Oh, do stop rambling, Eglantine. He's not my gentleman, and I don't wish to marry him. Not across the border or in Westminster Abbey. Contrary to my father's intentions I didn't come to Town to find a husband."

"So you say." This reply sounded rather singsong, almost as if it were a retort Eglantine had chanted on more than one previous occasion to Eleanor.

"Well, it's true," Eleanor protested. "You know very well that I only came to Town because it was the easiest way to leave the downs."

"And romance isn't part of your plan. You'll travel and see the world and never answer to anyone but yourself. Yes. Yes, so you've told me countless times before. But, you know, Eleanor, I almost wonder if the reason you say it isn't actually to convince yourself."

"That's ridiculous."

"Maybe not. Love isn't something you can control, you know. Have you ever thought of that? It isn't one of those decisions you can be in charge of. It just happens, and when love pleads admission to your heart, it can't be denied," she said, quoting a line from a novel she'd perused at the lending library. "Tell me, Eleanor, didn't your heart beat just a little faster when he swept you into his arms? Didn't you feel for one moment that there might be something more between the two of you? Beyond that time and place? That somehow he was a part of your life that couldn't be denied?"

"Yes," was Eleanor's reluctant admission. "My heart did beat faster, but it was probably nothing more than the storm and nearly crashing on the staircase and breaking a limb."

"Pah! That's not it at all. If only you'd admit that you're not really meant for that independent life you prattle on about. You're meant for love and romance. Why, Eleanor, you've found the man of your dreams."

"Your dreams, perhaps. But not mine. In my dreams, he sets me free."

"Don't utter such fustian. You'll never find satisfaction or happiness in freedom. You'll never be truly content until you find your other half." A slight frown wrinkled Elgantine's brow. "You don't suppose he's already married, do you?"

"He couldn't be. He kissed me." At this revelation a familiar warmth heated Eleanor's face, and, seeing her reflection in the pier glass, she wished she hadn't pinched her cheeks. She also wished that she hadn't told Eglantine about the kiss, for now her friend would surely believe she had found love. But Elgantine's reaction was not the enthusiastic affirmation of romance Eleanor anticipated.

"Oh, of course, a kiss. That clarifies everything," Eglantine murmured in quiet response to Eleanor's assumption that a kiss meant he was a bachelor. No matter what Eleanor assumed, Eglantine remained unconvinced about the precise meaning of that kiss. Even Eglantine, the romantic dreamer, knew that some married men kissed

women other than their wives. Her frown deepened. She liked Eleanor a great deal. Her friend
was witty and not at all missish, and she admired
the dignified manner in which Eleanor faced ad-
versity. On the other hand, Eleanor was hopelessly
in the woods on most facts of life, and it troubled
Eglantine that anyone could seem so mature about
some things while at the same time be woefully
ignorant of the ways of the world, particularly
those regarding courtship and romance. Maybe
that was why she liked Eleanor. Eglantine was a
twin, the unmarried and flightier half of the pair,
and while her sister Edith had always accused Eglantine of being cork-brained, with Eleanor she
could be the sensible one.

"You don't sound convinced," said Eleanor.

"I'm not. Not all gentlemen are what they appear." Eglantine knew this from devastating personal experience. Once she had imagined herself
leagues in love with the church organist at home
in Fleet Regis. Mr. Pratt, seemingly mild of manner and who had expressed sincere admiration for
the sonnets she composed, had, it developed, been
a French spy. This deflating chapter in Eglantine's
young life had, however, been ameliorated this
winter by the dowager duchess's invitation to
sponsor her for the Season, and Eglantine hardly
dwelled upon the bogus Mr. Pratt anymore.

"Of course he was a *gentleman*," Eleanor asserted. "It was obvious by his manner."

"A gentleman? Oh, no, Eleanor. Not *that*," jested
Eglantine. "Have you so soon forgotten Great-
Aunt Margaret's advice? Only a rogue will do. Not
a gentleman." She draped a shawl about her
shoulders, then wagged a teasing finger. "But fear
not, dear friend, I believe you're in luck, for no
gentleman would have dared steal a kiss as he did.
So a rogue he is after all."

Eleanor frowned and picked up her shawl, a

beautiful Indian cashmere with a pattern of pea-
cock feathers in blue and green and gold. She
didn't like this conversation. It was ridiculous to
talk about whether or not the gentleman was married. It didn't matter. Again she wished she hadn't
told Eglantine about that kiss. It was bad enough
not to be able to get that kiss off her mind without
having Eglantine attach all variety of consequence
to it.

"Why the sad face? Finding a rogue should be
superlative news."

"It's nothing but nonsense, Elgantine. Furthermore, all your prittle-prattle makes me think of
my father. I've no intention of having anything to
do with any man who might be like him."

"Oh, Eleanor, you mustn't be such a goose, and
don't pull such a long face. At least you're considering intentions toward some variety of gentleman. That's a step in the right direction."
Eglantine gave Eleanor a hug. "I was only teasing.
Truth to tell, it's high time you were kissed. The
Season's halfway through and Great-Aunt Margaret says that it's all right to have been kissed at
least once or twice. She said kissing is quite pleasurable, and . . ." Here, although there was no one
else in the bedchamber, Eglantine's voice dropped
to a conspiratorial whisper. ". . . I quite agree,
don't you?"

"That's the worst of it," said Eleanor. "Don't
you see? I did like it, and I can't stop thinking
about it."

"And what's wrong with that?"

"It's shameful. Proper young ladies don't dwell
upon such matters."

"Nor do proper young ladies talk of independence or turn down Lord Gatcombe after their
papa has given his blessing. I think that's only an
excuse, Eleanor. There's nothing wrong in thinking
about him, you know."

"But perhaps it was only the circumstance of the storm that made my heart beat faster. Somehow that troubles me more than my reaction. Perhaps it wasn't him or the kiss."

"And, of course, you'd rather it was the storm. Admitting that any man might affect your heart would rather muck up your plans," Eglantine said. She ignored the vexed expression this statement elicited from Eleanor and added, "I suppose it shall prey upon your mind forever. Haunt you. Unless, of course, you were to encounter him once again; then you would be able to gauge whether your reaction was the same or not."

"I suppose that might succeed." Kisses and romance and the frantic pounding of one's heart were mysteries to Eleanor, and she had to rely upon Eglantine's experience in this matter.

"Suppose! Why, of course it shall succeed," Eglantine said with a strong note of encouragement, having decided that Eleanor's only chance for happiness rested with the tall blue-eyed gentleman. To add the final irrefutable touch to her argument, she concluded, "The choice is yours, Eleanor. You can spend the rest of your days thinking about that kiss, or you can decide to search him out and satisfy yourself that it was nothing more than the storm."

"How clever you are, Eglantine. You knew I couldn't resist such an argument. And I shall do it, though it's a rather wicked thing to consider."

"Rather tame, I'd say. Oh, Eleanor, if you only knew the wicked things that normally and perfectly respectable young ladies have been known to do in pursuit of a gentleman."

"I'm not pursuing him," Eleanor corrected with a smile. She was pleased with her decision, and although she rather suspected Eglantine's motives, nothing would deter Eleanor once her mind had been made up.

"No, of course not," Eglantine appeased. She would have to be more cautious if she hoped to effect romance between Eleanor and the gentleman.

The strains of a lively gavotte could be heard from downstairs. Her grace's guests were arriving, dancing had commenced, and the young ladies made their way down the corridor toward the merriment below.

The party was a disaster. It wasn't the first unpleasant evening Eleanor had experienced during the Season, but somehow it seemed far worse than those other occasions when gay young people swirled about her, laughing and conversing as if she were nothing more than a speck of dust on the moiré-covered wall. It wasn't the first time her dance card had gone unsigned by anyone below the age of sixty, nor the first time she'd overheard disagreeable remarks about her father, or spent hours on the sidelines with a clutch of dowagers, who tolerated her as one might an indigent relation. But it was the first time that any of this hurt Eleanor, and she didn't understand why.

It was nearing midnight when the Duke of Yarmouth approached Eleanor. "Might I have the honor of your company for supper, Lady Eleanor?" he inquired in an over-loud voice. His grace was frightfully hard of hearing and had the unfortunate habit of assuming everyone else was as well.

"Thank you, your grace. I should like that." She accepted the duke's arm, and they strolled into the dining room where the great mahogany table had been removed and a myriad of smaller round tables had been arranged with Belgian linens and candelabras to accommodate parties of two and three.

"Her grace had always presented a superlative collation. Don't know how I survived those years when she wasn't entertaining. Quite missed her eel. You do like eel, don't you, m'dear? And the pigeon. The pickled eggs. It's quite divine."

"Yes, your grace." Eleanor didn't like eel or pickled eggs, and she shuddered. She didn't know what was worse: the fact that the duke's loud speech had attracted every eye in the dining room or the revolting manner in which the elderly gentleman piled his plate with excessive servings of every dish on the sideboard. There were platters heaped with lobster and shrimp, lamb and beef and veal, and an endless variety of puddings and custards and pastries, and the duke was going to partake of it all.

"Ain't got much appetite," he remarked with a sideways glance at the paltry helping of roast chicken and poached peaches Eleanor had served herself. "Not healthy for a young lady, y'know. Ain't one of those modern gels concerned about her figure, are you?"

"No, your grace." Eleanor stood as close to the duke as she could so that he might hear her reply without having to raise her voice. They walked toward one of the small tables. "It's just that I've kept country hours for so long I'm still unaccustomed to eating so late at night."

"Ah, yes. Yes. Quite so. Only just arrived in Town. Mulgrave's daughter, aren't you?"

Two footmen appeared to help seat the duke and Eleanor, and conversation halted at the surrounding tables. There was nothing so tempting as gossip, and the mention of Mulgrave in the presence of his daughter was tantalizing. How would the chit react? Would she show the proper shame?

"Yes, your grace, and my mother was Lady Penelope."

"Ah, yes. Yes. Lady Penelope. Believe I knew your mother. Sir Christopher Verney's gel, wasn't she? Your mother, you say. Haven't seen her for a while. How is Lady Penelope, by the by?"

"She's dead, your grace."

"What was that?"

"My mother is deceased," Eleanor said, aware that the couple to her right was hanging upon her every word. She loathed gossips and eavesdroppers, and although she knew it was highly improper, she couldn't help herself from adding in a voice that was just a tad too low for the duke to hear, but just loud enough for the nearest eavesdroppers, "My father killed her."

"The cheek of the girl!" exclaimed the lady seated behind Eleanor. A round of gasps circulated through the dining room, and someone else declared, "Shameless creature!"

"Ah, yes. Yes," remarked the duke. Although he hadn't been able to hear Eleanor's precise reply, he had heard the gasps and deduced that he'd made one of his usual gaffes. He replied with the sort of thing that generally sufficed for appropriate in most situations, "Should have known that, shouldn't I? Ah, well, nothing to be done about it, can there? Come now, eat up." And he set to attacking his supper with zeal, oblivious to the excited chatter surrounding him.

Eleanor stared at her chicken, regretting the impulse that had made her say such a thing. Her father's vile reputation was well-known, but that didn't matter. Her behavior had been ill-mannered. She was shameless. And the entire room was discussing her as if she weren't there.

"Whatever could have possessed the chit to suggest such a thing to his grace?"

"Bold as day."

"Without a shred of shame."

"You don't suppose it's bad blood? Like father, like daughter?" this from Lady Soames, who was seated behind Eleanor. "I'm so relieved my Henry

decided not to dance with her." Henry was Lady
Soames's middle son, a spotty-faced young man
who was much under the thumb of his mama.
"Despite it all, Lady Eleanor is a rather comely
creature, and Henry can be weak-minded when it
comes to such things."

"Indeed, Lady Soames, you're right. If not your
Henry, some other poor fool is bound to be taken
by those looks sooner or later," hissed a turbanned
creature.

"She's not marriage material, though. Thank
God," praised Lady Soames in a histrionic swoon.

"Indeed, who would want Vile Villiers as a
father-in-law?"

"I suppose I could tolerate Henry setting up an
establishment in St. John's Wood. At least I
wouldn't have to admit her to my drawing room
or acknowledge her in the park."

"Henry or whoever. St. John's Wood is the best
the chit will ever do."

Eleanor stared at the slice of roast chicken upon
her plate and willed herself to raise her head to
meet Lady Soames's regard. But she couldn't do it.
What they had said hurt too much, and Eleanor
couldn't budge for fear that she might do something to bring more attention to herself and make
matters worse. Of course, she scolded herself, it
shouldn't bother her what they said. Not one iota.
Eleanor wasn't looking for a match, and she
shouldn't care what any of those spiteful creatures
had to say about her. Then why did it hurt so?
Why was there a hollow aching spot in the pit of
her stomach that she couldn't control?

She glanced at the duke. He was absorbed in eel
and hadn't heard a word that had been said. He
caught her glance.

"Superb eel, m'dear." He pointed a fork at her
plate. "Do eat your peaches."

The last thing she wanted was food, and she responded with a polite nod as the duke went back to his eel and the malicious gossip continued.

"Speaking of St. John's Wood, have you heard the latest about Fortune?" inquired Lady Soames, who could be relied upon to know all the latest tattle.

"About to puff it off to the papers?" suggested Sir Charles Edenton.

"Hardly, Sir Charles. Surely you know, Lord Fortune has vowed never to wed," clarified Lady Adelaide Spencer. She was a rouged young bride in dampened magenta muslin, whose husband ought to have kept her under tighter rein.

"Fortune says he's not interested in marriage to anyone. Not now or ever."

"Why marry, when you can sample the charms of any lady you like?" simpered the rouged bride.

"Speak for yourself, Lady Adelaide," snapped Lady Soames.

"Fortune? Vowed never to wed?" repeated Sir Charles in disbelief. "Wherever did you ladies get such a notion? I knew the gentleman's father. Certainly he intends to carry on the family name."

"It's well-known, sir, Lord Fortune's heart is as black and cold as the Irish Sea."

"There's always an arrangement of convenience."

"For those who own a shred of conscience," sniffed Lady Soames. "Which Fortune lacks in spades. Hadn't you heard? He cuckolded Atherton, then merely wounded him in a duel and walked away. Oh, the shame. The shame," she ended with a series of scandalized tuts.

Eleanor had never heard of Lord Fortune, and with a name like that she supposed that he was probably some trumped-up cit. Still she couldn't help feeling sorry for the man. No one could be as bad as Lady Soames described, and he certainly didn't deserve to be the victim of the woman's evil tongue any more than she herself did.

The music began again, and couples drifted out of the dining room. The duke set his fork aside.

"Would you care to dance, Lady Eleanor?"

Eleanor didn't wish to dance, nor to be on the floor where all eyes might see her, or to have her toes crushed and be subjected to the duke's no doubt eely breath, but politeness dictated that she accept. And as they strolled from the dining room a thought rose unbidden in Eleanor's mind. How would the tall blue-eyed gentleman dance? Could he waltz? she wondered, recalling the pleasant scent of lime and how he had reacted when she touched that tiny half-moon scar beneath his eye. Her cheeks warmed at the memory, and Eleanor knew that Eglantine was right. She'd better find him quickly, and satisfy herself as to the reasons for her unaccountable reactions. The sooner she did that, the sooner she would be able to return her attention to the question of how and when to quit her father's household.

Five

THE YOUNG LADY'S sweet light laughter, her Gypsy black hair, that parting smile and that look of first-awakened passion haunted Litchfield. It wasn't at all like him to speculate for more than a few hours about a lost interlude. No woman was that important, or that desirable. To give so much consideration to a woman he didn't even know was, he decided, a definite sign of boredom, and as a curative, he threw himself into a blaze of wenching and gaming and drinking that would have killed most men.

A fortnight passed. He divested himself of Lady Maria Putney, took up residence with a ballet dancer, survived a carriage wreck on the Dover Road with a mere bruise to his shoulder, and lost and then won five thousand pounds at Crockford's hazard table. The Gypsy beauty he'd kissed that stormy afternoon was a faded memory, never to concern him again, until one afternoon when he found himself lurking about the giraffes on the staircase in the entrance hall of the British Museum.

He hadn't planned it, or at least he hadn't been aware of any conscious consideration to search for her, yet there he was at this ideal vantage point from which to observe all visitors as they entered.

He was groomed to perfection, wearing his newest bottle green waistcoat from Weston's, his pristine white neckcloth was tied *en cascade*, and he was paying no attention whatsoever to the towering pair of stuffed beasts, searching, instead, for a young lady with Gypsy black hair.

"Naturally there's a perfectly logical explanation why you haven't seen him," Eglantine consoled Eleanor. The young ladies had visited the British Museum and its environs every afternoon for the past two weeks, but to no avail. They had combed the exhibit halls and lurked about the shops and alleys up and down Great Russell Street, but there had been no sign of any tall blue-eyed gentleman. "Mayhap he was a tourist in the Metropolis. He didn't have an accent, did he?" Eglantine inquired, thinking that it would be the height of divine for Eleanor to have been kissed by a Russian prince or an American privateer. "Or perhaps he was called to his country seat on family business. An ailing relative or some such pressing duty." Eglantine paused to consider the possibilities. Truth to tell, there might be some less noble reason, and before she could stop herself, she blurted out, "You don't think he's a felon, do you? Perhaps he's a notorious highwayman wanted for murder and forced to go into hiding."

"Even I would not consider anything so utterly preposterous," Eleanor retorted as they strolled arm-in-arm through the museum's double door of carved oak and into a lofty entrance hall paved with Portland stone and grey marble. They were about to ascend the staircase and make their usual circuit of the exhibit rooms when a tiny squeak escaped Eleanor.

"What is it?" inquired Eglantine. "Is he here? Do you see him?"

Eleanor nodded.

Eglantine glanced about the entrance hall. It couldn't be the portly gentleman admiring a marble presentation of Shakespeare to her right, nor the schoolboys with a dour-faced tutor to her left. Then she looked up the staircase where a pair of stuffed giraffes loomed over an assortment of other animals from foreign lands, and she gasped in a manner worthy of the most flamboyant thespian.

"Oh, Eleanor, your gentleman *is* handsome. And to think that he kissed you. Oh, I may swoon at the thought."

Eleanor, however, did not hear this vulgar remark as she took in the sight of the gentleman, who was as tall and fair and masculine as she recalled. Engaged in reading a bronze explanatory placard, he hadn't noticed Eleanor, and she backed away from the staircase to catch her breath.

"Eleanor!" hissed Eglantine for the third time. "What do you intend to do? Do you want me to stay? Perhaps you should stumble on the staircase so he can rescue you once again."

"Yes. No. Oh, I don't know."

The gentleman looked up from the placard, and Eleanor averted her gaze, paying extraordinary attention to the introductory page of the official museum guide she had purchased with her admittance ticket.

"I could pretend to leave. But I could actually stay for a while, and if you needed me, I'd be in one of the other galleries," suggested Eglantine, who fervently hoped her friend would not do anything to upset the natural course of romance that was bound to unfold this afternoon.

"No, you don't have to do that." From the corner of her eye, Eleanor saw the gentleman descending the staircase. He was coming toward her, and her heart beat a deafening tattoo. Eleanor knew she and Eglantine were behaving like common shop girls. That's why her heart was beating so furiously. This entire search was beyond redemption. She deserved every one of Lady Soames's unkind words. Even the dowager duchess wouldn't approve. She and Eglantine should stop gaping at him and walk the other way. At the very least, they should cut him dead should he dare to speak to them. Proper young ladies of the *ton* did not acknowledge strange gentlemen, and they certainly did not seek them out. It was appallingly bold to remain where she was.

But Eleanor didn't wish to behave in a proper and ladylike fashion. She had already been deemed beyond the pale by polite society. What did it matter? Besides, this was her choice, and if she wished to make free choices, she must accept the full consequences. There could be no harm in talking to him. After all, that's what she had been hoping for these past two weeks. All she would do was see how she reacted in his presence. Of course, she'd thank him again for rescuing her. That would be all. Nothing more. And so she told Eglantine:

"Go ahead. Leave. You don't have to wait. Have the coachman Tom Pease drive you home, if you like. Then send him back to wait for me."

Although Eglantine was glad for an excuse to quit the museum, she did not budge. How perfect it would be to observe romance unfold between her friend and this divine gentleman. She did not like to miss that. Besides, what if Eleanor lost her courage?

"Are you sure you want me to leave?" Eglantine asked.

"Quite sure." Eleanor shooed Eglantine toward the double door.

"All right," was Eglantine's reluctant farewell as she turned to leave.

No sooner had she departed the entrance hall than the gentleman was standing before Eleanor.

Despite the boldness of her presence, Eleanor could not look up from the museum guide. She heard the gentleman cough. Her gloved hands seemed oddly clammy.

"Good morning, miss." He spoke in a whisper that was far too intimate, far too penetrating.

"Hello," came Eleanor's breathless reply. Her hands were definitely clammy. She wasn't reacting at all the way she had expected, and, gripping the pamphlet, she looked up. He was grinning at her.

"Do you recognize me without the greatcoat?" he asked, knowing that the twinkle in his blue eyes never failed to captivate the weaker sex. Holding his beaver hat in one hand, he executed a small bow after which he straightened up to regard her face and form. That grin deepened. While he had admired the young lady he'd kissed during the storm, he quite fancied the blushing creature who stood before him. She was even lovelier than he recalled, her hair blacker and her ruby lips more kissable, and an eagerness to make her his was rekindled.

"Of course I remember you, sir," she said, noticing with the most absurd sense of relief that he didn't have that pinched and stuffed look resulting from a starched high-pointed collar and nipped frock coat that was affected by dandies.

Silence ensued, and he shifted his weight from one foot to the other. Eleanor continued to hold the pamphlet with both clammy hands. Her heart was racing. *It had been him,* not the storm. She honestly hadn't expected this. Eleanor was unprepared, and she didn't know what to do. Run and hide was her first thought, then she reminded herself about accepting the consequences of her decisions, and she knew she couldn't flee, nor could she be rude. After all, the gentleman had rescued her. She had to be polite, she told herself.

"Do you come here often, miss?"

Eleanor started. "Whenever it's open." She was thankful for this idle talk. Her breathing was becoming more even. "And you, sir, do you visit often?"

"Not as much as I'd like. I'd no idea there were such pretties on display."

She nodded. The meaning of his words had escaped her. There was another silence.

At length, Eleanor asked, "Are you a scholar, sir?"

"A scholar? No." He was taken aback that someone might mistake him for a scholar. It was preposterous. The Earl of Litchfield, notorious rakehell, gamester, and more commonly known as Lord Fortune, a scholar! Evidently, she didn't have the vaguest clue who he was, and to think that she'd never even heard of Lord Fortune pleased him. If she were familiar with his character, it might ruin his chance at seduction. For that's what this second encounter was truly about. Finding her again wasn't about discovering her name and getting to know who she was by indulging in sentimental dialogue. It was about having his way with her.

"Allow me to introduce myself. Addison Weare, at your service, my lady." He omitted his title and observed her expression. There still were no signs of recognition. "Might I accompany you through the exhibit?" He offered his arm.

She was going to say no, but the oddest thing occurred. She had the clearest image of that horrendous supper with the Duke of Yarmouth. She wasn't sure why she thought of that awful evening at this precise moment or why it made her respond with a pretty smile. Contrary to her own best intentions, she slipped her arm in his.

"I'd like that immensely, and I'm very happy to meet you, Mr. Weare. I'm Miss Carew. Miss Nora Carew," said Eleanor. She didn't dare tell him her real name. She didn't want him to know she was Mulgrave's daughter. And so she told him her name was Nora Carew. Nora because that had been Lady Penelope's pet name for her; Carew because it was the author's name that sprang off the printed page of the museum guide.

"Ah, Carew. You're Welsh," he drawled. "I should have known with those wild black curls."

She blushed. Mr. Weare's voice caused the unbidden image of being cloaked in nothing else but velvet to rise across her mind's eye, and her thick dark lashes fluttered against ivory skin as she averted her gaze from his. Unbeknownst to Eleanor, she presented a charming sight.

"And you're modest, too," Mr. Weare added. "Hasn't anyone told you you're a beauty, Miss Nora Carew?"

"Does one's mother count?" she whispered and peered up from beneath lowered lashes for his response.

He chuckled at her delightful wit and open nature. This seduction was going to be an easy one, and with a confident, almost smug grin he led her back up the stairs and past the giraffes. "No, mothers don't count. It will, however, be my distinct pleasure to make up for such an unfortunate oversight and remind you of your rare fairness as often as I can." He paused on the threshold of the natural history exhibit to take her gloved hands in his.

"Now to the remedy, Miss Carew." Looking down at her upturned face, he whispered, "Your eyes are like stars in the southern sky, hinting of unlocked secrets and beckoning my soul to unknown adventures. And your hair, so wild and dark, begs freedom, Miss Carew. How I should

like to take off that bonnet and loosen it." His
voice dropped to a husky undertone. "How I
should like to see those wild raven locks cascade
down your back like—"

Eleanor snatched her hands away. "You mustn't
say such things, sir, or I shall start believing you."

"Don't you like it?" While he believed such
flowery compliments were ridiculous, most
women he had known appreciated them. Truth to
tell, the business about taking off her bonnet and
freeing her hair had affected the seduction of more
than one female.

"Of course I like it. What young lady wouldn't?
But such compliments seem dangerous, for I
might get an exceedingly swollen head and lose
all grasp of reality."

"That's rather the point." He flashed a grin, entirely aware of the disarming effect it had on the
weaker sex.

Eleanor knew an unsettling pang deep inside
her. It was a feminine reaction, marking her
awareness of him as a man, and her knees became
as weak as they had been when he'd kissed her.
She took a tiny step away from him. Sweet
heaven, her reactions were the same as before. Only this time they were much more vivid,
quicker and more intense. Eleanor was confused,
and, remembering Eglantine's suggestion that he
might be a rogue, she observed him with a sharp
eye.

"Are you trying to seduce me, Mr. Weare?"

Egad, the chit was forthright. Even the most experienced flirts, skilled in the art of suggestion and
nuance, were never so direct. He regarded her in
amusement. There was nothing about Miss Carew
to suggest the slightest familiarity with seduction.
She was an innocent who'd probably been fed a
litany of horror stories by some prig of a govern-
ess. She was an original, and he smiled, liking

more and more what he saw before him. "That's a rather unseemly question, Miss Carew."

"So is seduction, Mr. Weare. Unseemly. Although I couldn't truly say, for I've no experience at such things, and my friend Lady Eglantine thinks I'm woefully ignorant. Actually, she called me witless. Not unkindly, of course, but she was rather on the—"

He raised a hand to stop her speech. "You're not witless, Miss Carew, not in the least. You are charming, and though it's not an appropriate topic, you're quite correct. Seduction *is* most unseemly, and yes, in response to your question—" He paused for the briefest moment, which seemed to Eleanor like an eternity. "—I was going to seduce you."

Eleanor's heart plummeted. He had told the truth, and for that she should have been thankful. But she wasn't. *Yes, I was going to seduce you.* That was the sort of behavior Eleanor attributed to a rogue. Seduction, Eleanor believed, implied deception and the selfish use of one individual by another. Only men as vile as her father engaged in seduction. Eleanor didn't want to be seduced. She merely wanted to know this man in order to understand why he caused her to experience such extraordinary reactions.

"You're frowning." He essayed a lighter tone. "I haven't offended you, have I?"

"No, you didn't offend me, and since you were honest in your response, I can be no less with you." She stood her ground looking very brave. Her chin trembled a smidge, and she clasped her hands together. She was the picture of nervous confusion, and, after a deep breath, she continued, "You didn't offend me, sir. You disappointed me. You see, I trusted you, and as I think seduction implies a measure of deceit, it appears my trust was misguided. It isn't pleasant to feel betrayed."

Whatever Litchfield had expected to hear, it wasn't this vulnerable confession, and of a sudden, he was ill at ease. He was used to being in control, but Miss Nora Carew, quite without trying, was managing to thoroughly discompose him. There was something in the way this particular young lady looked at him that caused him to pause, and although he couldn't put his finger on what it was, the effect was boggling. He wanted this woman, perhaps more than any other, but not so soon, not now, and not regardless of the consequences. It was deuced peculiar. He'd never been ambivalent like this. He'd always taken what he wanted. Lord Fortune had never possessed an ounce of conscience. He didn't have the foggiest notion what to make of Miss Carew. She was a confounding wench. Frightfully disconcerting. And so were his reactions.

"Well, Miss Carew, if I promise not to seduce you, could we be friends? Or try to be, at least?" Litchfield was stunned to hear himself make this proposal, and those startling words seemed to echo in mockery through the vaulted exhibit room. Had he lost his mind to give up so easily? There wasn't a female in London who wasn't his for the taking. Or was there?

"Friends?" came her guarded reply. Her intention had been to see him only this once, and although she did not like the discovery that he could discompose her with a glance, she had also discovered that she enjoyed his company. He was clever and intelligent. And he had been honest. If she could be friends with Eglantine, why not with this gentleman? It was her choice, and she rather liked the idea of doing something unexpected. Up until now, there had been a logical quality to her choices, but not in this case.

"I think we might try," she said.

"Only think?" He was taken aback. What more

could any young lady expect? Egad, his offer was tantamount to pledging the existence of a eunuch. Hell, if he knew what it was that Miss Nora Carew wanted! Probably too much, and if he had any sense, he'd walk away from her and never look back.

"There's one other thing, sir, before we might be friends," she stated in a tone so earnest he was further disarmed. "You aren't married, are you?"

He burst out laughing. "No, I'm not married, Miss Carew."

"What's so funny?" She pursed those luscious red lips.

"I have the oddest feeling you're taking over my life," he said, struggling against the urge to break his promise and kiss her right then and there in broad daylight before some gaggle of offended tourists.

"It's not my intention, sir, to take over your life," she apologized. Had she any inkling of the direction of his thoughts, she wouldn't have been able to meet his gaze as she did.

"I didn't think it was," he replied with a reassuring smile as he escorted her into the exhibition.

The next two hours were passed strolling through the various saloons dedicated to zoology. They lost all track of time and were surprised when the closing bell chimed.

"Goodness, I'd no notion of the time. I must be on my way," Eleanor said. "Thank you for a pleasant afternoon, Mr. Weare."

"May I escort you home, Miss Carew?"

"No, thank you. My coachman is waiting for me." She couldn't let him know where she lived. She couldn't let him discover she wasn't Nora Carew, but the daughter of the Earl of Mulgrave. She didn't want to see the inevitable disdain on his face.

"When will you be back?" he asked as they retraced their footsteps to descend the staircase and pass the giraffes.

"Tomorrow," she said. There was an odd raspiness in Eleanor's voice that made her sound not at all like her usual self, and she couldn't help hoping that he would be here again.

"Might I have the honor of taking you to tea, Miss Carew? There's a small establishment around the corner. Quite respectable, and I'm told the proprietor serves an excellent strawberry tartlet."

"I should like that." She accepted his invitation in a demure manner that gave no hint of the way her heart soared.

They reached the museum entrance, exited through the grand double door, and she was about to step off the portico when his voice stopped her.

"Before you go . . ."

"Yes?" She looked at him.

"Since I answered your question about whether or not I was married, would you be so kind to answer one for me?"

"If I can."

Something had been on Litchfield's mind for the past two hours, and if he didn't ask, it would plague him. He had to know.

"Have you ever thought about traveling, Miss Carew? About seeing where all of this came from?"

Her reply began as laughter. It was a melody of sheer delight. Dots of pink colored her cheeks. Her smile was open, and her eyes sparkled with a touch of mischief. "Of course I've thought about such things, Mr. Weare. I'd adore to travel the world. It's my greatest wish, and though I'm sure you'll think me quite a contrary female, I must confess that I'd adore to have such adventures. Even at the expense of a Season or marriage. If we're to be friends, you must know I'm quite hopeless about such things. I've even dreamed of sailing on a pirate ship to faraway isles."

Lord Litchfield, who maintained tight control over his emotions, experienced the most extraordinary response to this declaration. It was an actual physical sensation, a sort of lurching somewhere in the region of his chest, and in that moment, Litchfield knew this forthright green chit was far more dangerous than the most world-weary demimondaine or the most marriage-minded ingenue. He could ward off threats to his pocketbook or to his bachelor status, but this singular young lady threatened something else.

He thought again that it would be best to walk away and forget about her once and for all. It was foolish to have come looking for her, absurd to have invited her to meet him for refreshments on the morrow, and even crazier to have made misguided promises of friendship—but looking at those golden-flecked eyes, those luscious red lips, and that enticing figure, he was lost.

Miss Nora Carew, Litchfield decided, would be well worth the risk.

Six

O VER THE NEXT three weeks, Eleanor and
Litchfield visited in the saloons of Montague
House every Tuesday and Thursday, concluding
each afternoon with tea and strawberry tarts at
The Bumblebee and Clover. On Wednesdays,
when the museum was closed to the public,
Litchfield orchestrated outings. There had been a
visit to Week's Mechanical Museum in Haymarket,
a sailing trip up the Thames past Hampton Court,
and now the couple was embarked on a carriage
ride northwest of the Metropolis on the Ealing to
High Wycombe Road.

"I believe, Miss Carew, you shall accuse me of
breaking my promise, but truly, you're a vision to
behold, and it would be a grievous wrong not to
tell you so," Litchfield said as he negotiated his
phaeton through a crush of city-bound farm wag-
ons. Everyone seemed to be heading into the Metropolis, while he and Eleanor had left the
vegetable gardens of Paddington and the final vestiges of London were fading behind them.

Eleanor was wearing an Angouleme walking
outfit, named for the daughter of Marie Antoinette
and popularized by the recent Bourbon Restora-
tion. The spencer, which was made of golden
brown satin and sported a high rolling collar, en-

hanced Eleanor's natural beauty. Her black curls
glistened like coal, her pure complexion would
have inspired poets to write of Devon cream, and
the golden highlights in her eyes were more pronounced than usual. She seemed to sparkle, and
framing this impression of vibrant beauty was a
satin hat trimmed with fleurs-de-lis in pearls and
a high fluted crown.

Litchfield smiled at the satisfying sight. "You're
rather like a golden sunrise. Yes, that's an apt de-
scription, I'd say. Gentle and delicate, not yet
awakened, but hinting at the hidden pleasures of a
glorious summer day."

"Indeed, sir!" Eleanor feigned high indignation
and lowered her lashes. Her cheeks warmed, not,
however, in response to this flirtatious remark, but
to her reaction. She was finding that she rather
liked it when he complimented her, rather enjoyed
it when her heart raced a bit and heat rushed to
her face.

Truth to tell, there were a lot of things about Mr.
Weare that she quite liked. The way he sat beside
her on the small bench at the corner table in The
Bumblebee and Clover was endearing, especially
when to sit opposite her would, of course, be the
proper thing to do. There were other things too. It
was thrilling to discover him staring at her when
she least expected it. And she would be disappointed if one day his lips ceased to linger a moment too long above her gloved hand when he
greeted her.

Eleanor was glad that she'd accepted his offer of
friendship. It was new and different, and, from
time to time, he even caused her to entertain the
most outrageous thoughts—in particular the exceedingly wicked and undeniably dangerous wish
that he might break his promise and kiss her
again. Only, of course, to see how she might react.
Such was not, however, possible. Mr. Weare had

been true to his word. There was nothing about his behavior that the innocent Eleanor could discern as seductive.

She tilted her head to one side and smiled. He was wearing a bright blue waistcoat that matched the color of his eyes, and as always he was looking devilishly handsome with his fair hair and slight tan. "That, sir, was indeed a dangerous compliment, and had you not warned me, I would certainly suspicion the honor of your intentions."

He chuckled, liking very much the change he sensed in her. While Miss Carew had always been forthright, there had been a hesitancy about her that was no longer there. He recalled their barge trip up the Thames to Hampton Court and how she had held back when he suggested she handle the boat's tiller. That hesitancy was gone now. There was a new confidence in her. She was blossoming, especially in the way she gave tit-for-tat in a teasing repartee such as this, and Litchfield liked to think he was in some small part responsible for that.

It appeared his plans were going as he wished. Although it was a circuitous route to the boudoir, allowing this friendship stuff to take its course looked like it was going to work. In the meantime, his desire for Miss Carew had not waned; if anything it had strengthened. Every time he looked at her his blood stirred. There was something special about her. No other woman had captured his amorous interest as much as Miss Carew, yet he hadn't broken his vow. He would not until he was certain success would be his, and perhaps, he mused, today was the day he would meet that success. Encouraged by this prospect, he grinned once again, and against the tan of his skin, his teeth were startlingly white and his eyes were a particularly bright blue. He gave the reins a flick, and the pair of matched chestnuts quickened their pace to a brisk trot.

The morning fog had burned off, the early summer sun blazed overhead, and a light breeze teased the uppermost branches of the trees, reminding Eleanor of the countryside near Mulgrave Manor. Of course, this narrow country lane wasn't really the same as the vast expanse of rolling Berkshire downs, but the air was fresh and the bleating lambs and crying rooks were more familiar than the sing-song of the flower girl below her window on Curzon Street or the midnight watch's echoing call.

"I had forgotten how much I like the countryside," Eleanor declared.

Litchfield cast a curious glance upon Miss Carew. She wasn't looking up at him, but was watching the passing scenery, and keeping one eye upon the road, he studied her expression in profile. She was happy, absurdly so, and again, he hoped that in some small way he was responsible.

"Oh, look," she exclaimed and pointed at a lad fishing in a nearby stream. The boy held up a string laden with iridescent sunfish, Eleanor waved and her smile widened. Turning back to Mr. Weare, she clarified her earlier remark. "These past weeks in Town have been very exciting for me, you understand. There have been so many novel things to see and do, but all in all I think I prefer the country." Expecting no reply, she resumed watching the scenery.

It was revealing comments such as that which piqued Litchfield's curiosity about Miss Carew. This was not the first time she had said something that made him wonder, *Who was Miss Nora Carew? Who were her family? Where had she come from? Where was this particular countryside that she favored over London? What secrets did she keep?* Although she didn't possess a title, there was nothing com-

mon about her. Even a scoundrel could recognize
that. Miss Carew was a lady born and bred, and
Litchfield couldn't help wondering about her. She
seemed to be at liberty to do as she wished.
Wasn't there someone somewhere concerned with
her welfare and the safety of her good name? Unless she told him, however, he'd never know.

It was one of his rules. No questions. To do so
would countenance an exchange on the subject of
their backgrounds and private lives, which was
much too messy. Besides, he'd never cared one
way or the other whether he knew much about
any female. Until this particular young lady, that
is. Still, rules were rules, and he couldn't ask. By
that same token, Litchfield *never* volunteered to
tell any woman about himself.

She said nothing more to enlighten him, and
Litchfield continued to study her from the corner
of one eye, wondering if he might find some clue
about Miss Carew in her delicate features, a resemblance, perhaps, to a parent or mayhap to an
elder sister. If he'd ever encountered another female who had Miss Carew's unique beauty, he
would remember her, which he didn't. And as for
a male relative, it was difficult to imagine any
gentleman with so creamy a complexion and such
inviting red lips.

Eleanor was acutely aware of Mr. Weare's scru-
tiny, and she forced herself to look straight ahead
as if nothing were out of the ordinary. She would
die before revealing how his regard made her
palms clammy and how funny little warm sensations churned through her stomach and her toes
curled in her satin slippers. It was often like this.
She could be looking at something in the museum
or pouring their tea at The Bumblebee and Clover,
and all the while she knew his gaze was fixed
upon her. Whenever Eleanor caught him staring at
her, her heart would beat a little faster. She would

remember those moments in the rain. She would know it was his effect upon her, not the storm's, and she would entertain dangerous thoughts.

It happened now, the memory, the dangerous thoughts, and the question "Might I drive the carriage?" popped forth from Eleanor without a moment's consideration.

One of Mr. Weare's eyebrows arched upward. "Do you know how to handle a high-spirited team such as this?" he asked, not in the least bit shocked by her request. He was amused.

"No," she confessed, feeling somewhat like a schoolgirl caught in a fib. Quite of their own accord, her lips pursed together in an expression that seemed to say, *But that doesn't mean I couldn't learn.*

Miss Carew's moue was adorable. So adorable, in fact, that Litchfield found it nearly impossible to resist her. Lord, but that luscious mouth wasn't made for kissing. It was made for plundering, and he wanted to taste its temptation. His body began to tighten. *Not now,* an inner voice warned. *Not until you're certain she won't protest.* Instead, he seized upon this opportunity to advance toward his ultimate goal. He grinned. "Then I shall be pleased to teach you the finer skills of a whip."

"I should like that. Thank you."

"You've got to come closer to me. Come now, closer. As close as you can get." He tried to hide his desire by sounding matter-of-fact. It wouldn't be wise to reveal his eagerness. He mustn't frighten her in any way.

Eleanor didn't hesitate to slide closer. She trusted Mr. Weare, and when he wrapped an arm about her waist she leaned against the support of his inner shoulder. That pleasant scent of lime and leather surrounded her once more. She liked that. It was very masculine, she thought, and in contrast, it made her feel exceedingly feminine.

"I'm ready for my first lesson," she said. There was a husky little catch in her voice.

"Good. We'll begin with a demonstration. Watch how I do it." He indicated the manner in which he held the reins in his hands, and after a few minutes, he transferred the ribbons from his grip to hers. "Hold firmly, but don't pull," he advised, demonstrating the technique of letting up on or tightening the tension. The team slowed its pace, and for the next miles Eleanor concentrated on driving until Litchfield remarked, "I believe you're a natural whip, Miss Carew."

"And you, sir, are a natural teacher," she returned the flattery. "Are you a member of the Four-in-Hand Club, Mr. Weare?" Eleanor referred to the exclusive driving club whose members dedicated themselves to the practice of their four-in-hand skills.

"No, for as I'm sure you know the trip to the Windmill in Salt Hill is executed single file and at a steady trot. Of course no passing is allowed. Conformity, not novelty, is the standard. Why, poor Tommy Onslow, whose coaching skills are second to none, was denied admittance merely because of an eccentric penchant for black cattle and somber black drag. I fear my reputation for racing would not engender favor among the venerable members."

"Racing? Don't tell me you've a fondness for racing, sir," teased Eleanor. There was a note of excitement in her voice which was matched by a telling glimmer in her eyes as she repeated, "Racing, you say."

Litchfield recognized the flash of something daring in her expression. She met his gaze, and he watched in fascination as those brown orbs turned to gold, her red lips parting in expectation.

"Are you considering what I think you are, Miss Carew?"

She managed an affirmative nod. He was having *that* effect upon her again, causing her to entertain the most extraordinary notions. Whenever she was with Mr. Weare, Eleanor dared to do things of which she had only dreamed. Sometimes she wasn't at all her normal self. She didn't consider decisions, she leapt to them, and this was one of those times. Of course, it was all his fault. Not hers in the least. She could still be entirely logical, if she chose. Giving a spirited toss of her head, she rejoined:

"And what is it that you imagine that I'm thinking, Mr. Weare?"

"You're thinking of racing, Miss Carew," he drawled with a dangerous grin. "I believe you'd like to speed down this lane. Fast as lightning. I believe you'd like to race this team as if the devil were at your heels. That's rather *dangerous*, wouldn't you say?"

She blushed. He'd read the direction of her thoughts as surely as if they'd been printed on the page of a book, and it didn't bother her one jot. This wasn't the first time he'd known what she was thinking, and the truth was, it was another one of those things she'd grown to like about Mr. Weare.

"Indeed, it *is* dangerous, Mr. Weare, but didn't you once tell me that there would be little to treasure in life if there was no risk?"

Litchfield chuckled. "I wasn't sure you'd recall that conversation." They were referring to a light-hearted debate in which they'd engaged at The Bumblebee and Clover on the subject of spontaneity.

"I remember *everything*, Mr. Weare," Eleanor said as if it were a challenge. Their gazes locked and held. "You told me there would be little to relish in life without risk. You told me you took risks all the time."

"And you told me you'd never risked anything, Miss Carew." He spoke as softly as she had. It was almost as if they were talking about something else. "But I think you'd like to change that."

She inhaled, and the country air scented by freshly mowed hay and wildflowers further intoxicated her. He was right. The notion of galloping down the lane, the wind tugging at her bonnet while the scenery sped past was intriguing. Twin dots of pink rose upon her cheeks, and she laughed. "Yes, in this instance, I should like to take that risk."

Before he could reply, she flicked the reins, the carriage lurched, and they were off, gaining speed as the road flattened for a stretch of about a quarter mile. It was better than Eleanor could have imagined. The wind whistled in her ears and she laughed as her satin bonnet sailed off and her hair came loose to tumble about her shoulders. It was exhilarating to feel such power and freedom. This was better than dancing in the rain in the courtyard at Mulgrave Manor. This experience was well worth the risk. She had never felt so alive, and when Eleanor glanced at Mr. Weare an instantaneous connection of energy and understanding leapt between them. Eleanor laughed with abandon, and she leaned against the support of his shoulder as they careened over the open road.

It was at moments like this that Litchfield damned his promise. He had long suspected, long hoped that Miss Carew's heart was as wild as those glossy black curls tumbling about her shoulders, and now he was certain it was true. She was a highly sensual creature, which led to the corollary conclusion that Miss Nora Carew was meant to know the physical delights a man might show a woman. Indeed, if she was a passionate woman, she would sooner or later surrender to some man, and Litchfield was determined that before much longer he would be that man.

Up ahead there was a sharp curve in the road. The horses were racing at a full gallop. They were going too fast for Eleanor to control them around the approaching bend.

"Here, let me take over," said Litchfield, and Eleanor surrendered the ribbons without argument. He brought the vehicle to a stop at the crest of a hill. The beasts were panting with exertion, so was Miss Carew as she looked from the sweep of pastureland before them toward Litchfield.

"Oh, my goodness. My goodness," came her breathless exclamation. She was radiant. Her cheeks were rosy, her eyes sparkled, and errant black curls prettily framed her flushed and smiling face. "I've never experienced anything like that before. Such speed, such—"

But the words were lost as Litchfield's mouth covered Eleanor's to capture what it was she would have said. His hands threaded through those soft dark curls, smoothing them away from her brow and cheeks, and tenderly, yet firmly, he held her face between the cradle of his palms. It was a demanding kiss, quite different from the one beneath the portico at the British Museum. For this time, there was no doubt in Eleanor's mind that it was Mr. Weare to which she was responding. Her heart raced, and something deep inside her was melting.

Then as suddenly at it began, it was over. He raised his head, and his clear blue gaze met her golden eyes.

"How I've wanted to do that," Litchfield murmured as he pushed a stray curl off her forehead. The other hand lingered at her temple. "I know I've broken my promise, but—"

"I wanted it too. I'm just as much to blame," came Eleanor's urgent whispered confession, and in the next instant, her hand rose to her mouth as if to snatch back the unguarded revelation. Her fingers trembled, her tongue darted out to moisten her passion-bruised lips, and for the first time, Eleanor was unsure of why it was she'd ever sought out Mr. Weare in the first place. She'd told herself it was only to find out why she had experienced such a peculiar reaction to him, but she hadn't been honest with herself.

Verily, she'd wanted more of his kisses. It appeared she possessed the nature of a wanton. And while Eleanor wondered how this could have happened, an inner voice reminded her that she was, after all, Vile Villiers's daughter. Who would expect anything else?

But what upset Eleanor even more than this was the nagging thought that perhaps Eglantine had been right about Mr. Weare all along. Perhaps her interest in Mr. Weare was more than curiosity or friendship or wanton lust. Perhaps this was romance. Perhaps she wasn't really meant for the dreams of independence she'd set for herself. These thoughts were thoroughly discomposing, and Eleanor struggled to hide her confusion.

Litchfield drank in the sight of her moist lips and the rapid rise and fall of her chest. The effect he had upon her was most pleasing, and he looked back to her eyes fully expecting to see them ablaze with the golden lights of passion. That, however, was not the case, and he was caught off guard, instead, by an expression of innocence and confusion. Of its own accord, his hand fell away from her temple.

As surely as he knew he would soon break his pledge not to seduce her, he knew that one way or another he was going to hurt Miss Carew. He'd never cared about such things before, and damnation, he wished he didn't care now. Truth to tell, he didn't want to hurt Miss Carew. On the other hand, he couldn't see any other way for it. She was far too exquisite not to claim for his own. He'd been a fool to let this friendship stuff go on for so long. He had to bring this liaison to its proper conclusion as quickly and with as little sentimentality as possible, for to wait any longer might mean she would never be his.

"Might I have the pleasure of your company this evening?" Litchfield asked. "Would you join me for the opera gala? *On dit* the Prussian Field Marshall Blucher will be in attendance. Perhaps even the Princess of Wales."

Eleanor's heart leapt. Thank goodness, he hadn't been repulsed by her admission of wanting that kiss. This was Mr. Weare's first invitation to something other than one of their daytime excursions, and she couldn't help wondering that if this was romance, should she accept or should she say no? Her initial instinct was to decline. She didn't want romance, but she'd never been a coward. Besides, it would be foolish to pretend that she didn't like the notion of dancing with him, perhaps even waltzing. This was, however, a hopeless fantasy. A dark vision of her father loomed in her mind. As well as the vision of a gloating Lady Soames. Eleanor didn't know which would be worse. Her father's certain anger if she were to accept the invitation of a gentleman he hadn't chosen for his daughter, or Lady Soames's spiteful delight should her father cause a public scene.

"I fear, sir, I must decline." She might not be a coward when it came to her own choices, but she'd rather avoid confrontation with her father, if at all possible.

"I see," was Litchfield's cool reply. Obviously, the kiss had been a mistake. He'd overplayed his hand today and had no one to blame but himself for this rebuff. He essayed a nonchalant shrug. "Ah, well, another time, perhaps."

"Oh, it's not that." Eleanor read his rejection and was eager to correct this mistaken impression. Her soft voice was laden with obvious regret. The golden highlights faded from her eyes. "It's not that I wouldn't like to accept your invitation. It's that I can't."

"A previous engagement?" Litchfield wondered aloud, knowing the most extraordinary and unfamiliar prick of jealousy. It was only a prick, but it was there nonetheless.

"Something like that," she replied in a bleak voice.

"What is it?" he asked. He was breaking the rules, asking personal questions, but he couldn't help it. Somehow this was important, perhaps even more important than himself and his own selfish ambition to bed Miss Carew. "You must tell me what's troubling you, for I would help you, if I might."

"If only it were that simple," was her wistful reply.

"Nothing is ever simple," he whispered. With one hand he took her chin between his thumb and forefinger to tilt her face upward. He dropped a quick tender kiss to the corner of each eye. At that precise moment he wanted nothing more from Miss Carew than to see her smile as she had when they embarked on this trip, to hear the sweet music of her laughter. "I would erase your unhappiness, if I could."

"You're very kind."

"No, I'm selfish," was his gruff retort. He didn't like weak sentimentality being attributed to him. It was alien. He didn't like feeling as if some stranger had crawled beneath his skin. She was getting to him. She was stirring up emotions he'd hidden for a long time, and he didn't like that.

"You're not selfish, if you would concern yourself with another's happiness." Mr. Weare didn't say anything to this gentle rejoinder, and Eleanor went on, "I'm not extravagant. It doesn't take much to make me happy. Simply spending these afternoons in your company is enough."

"What, no champagne?" He was taken aback that someone would want him and nothing more. "No ruby ear bobs? No sable cloaks or diamond bracelets?" He put one hand over hers. "Is that all you ask?"

"And that you rescue me."

Egad, she wasn't proposing, was she? He controlled the instinct to snatch his hand away. He'd no intention of being caught in a parson's mousetrap. Surely that wasn't where Miss Carew thought this was going. She couldn't be *that* naive, could she? "Excuse me?"

Eleanor giggled at Mr. Weare's gaping expression. "Rescue me. Take me to that pirate ship we talked of and sail with me to the farthest corner of the earth."

"Ah, escape," he said with notable relief. "You wish to run away from whatever it is that's troubling you. I can understand that."

She cast him a quizzical glance that begged explanation, but he was looking straight ahead with a closed expression that didn't encourage query.

He picked up the ribbons, set the pair of chestnuts to a trot, and they rode the next mile in silence. At length, Litchfield spoke.

"A pirate ship, you say. Would another sailing outing suffice instead? We could go out in a larger boat. A friend of mine keeps a small yacht for day outings. I'm sure he'd let us borrow it, and we can sail past Allhallows into the Mouth of the Thames and along the coast. It's quite a different experience compared to the Thames about Hampton Court Palace. We might even get wet, if the wind whips up and the sea is running high. Just the sort of thing for a pirate and his lady," he ended with a smile.

"That sounds a superlative alternative. You're a true friend, Mr. Weare," Eleanor said. "I should have known I could rely upon you."

This elicited a sensation of weakness in Litchfield's stomach, and he considered Miss Carew's statement in an increasingly distempered mood. It was painfully obvious that she trusted him, and in response, his conscience began to whisper, *You can't dishonor that trust. You can't hurt Miss Carew. You can't seduce her. Can't seduce her. Can't seduce her.*

His grip on the ribbons tightened, and, in a mounting anger born of frustration, he urged the team to a gallop. Litchfield was willing to accept that this would not be the day he met success with Miss Carew, but damnation, he didn't like thinking that it might never come to pass.

When had he started thinking of her in terms more serious than a soft body to pass a lonely night? It couldn't be that his intentions were honorable, could it? He wasn't sure. All he knew was that he wouldn't be satisfied with only one night with Miss Carew, and that he wasn't willing to risk that one night at the price of losing her altogether.

Seven

"ONLY A FEW more minutes, Miss Carew, and we'll be there," Litchfield assured her as the vehicle in which he and Eleanor were riding made its way through the hamlet of Tilbury. The *Windsong*, a pleasure yacht which Litchfield had won from Sir Anthony Howitt in a game of hazard, was berthed in this village twenty-six miles downstream from London, and this morning, Litchfield's coachman had made the trip in record time. "It hasn't been a bad ride, has it?"

"Not atall. I always enjoy our chats, and your tales of river pirates and mudlarks were most amusing. If only half of what you said is true, then I'm quite glad this is now and not a hundred years ago." Eleanor craned her neck for a better view of the river. It was wider here, much wider, and the water was as black as ink and running fast to the sea. Ferries worked their way back and forth between Tilbury and Gravesend on the opposite shore, and the skyline beyond the village rooftops was a jumble of masts and sails. "I'm surprised to see so many vessles this far downstream," remarked Eleanor.

"The tide is about to turn," Litchfield said as if it sufficed for explanation.

"Mr. Weare, I thought you knew by now that

with the exception of our outing to Hampton
Court, my entire experience with watercraft is lim-
ited to the dinghy in the millpond at home. Mention of the turning tide makes no sense to me."

Litchfield grinned. He liked the saucy way Miss
Carew had said *Mr. Weare*. It was almost as if they
were the oldest of bosom bows. He expanded,
"This is the last of the river's deep waterway
quays. Many of these ships have made their way
here from the wharfs at Queenhithe or the Isle of
Dogs to sail out on the tide to meet the sea just as
we shall."

"To meet the sea. That's rather poetic, Mr.
Weare." Again there was that saucy tone in her
voice, and a playful smile that set her brown eyes
dancing with golden highlights. "You know, this
will be the first time I shall see the sea," Eleanor
said, part confession, almost a whisper, her voice
trembling with quiet excitement.

"You're not frightened?"

"Frightened? Of course not." From beneath the
brim of her Oldenburg bonnet, Eleanor peered at
Mr. Weare a bit more closely. The gold in her eyes
dimmed, then regained its splendor. "There isn't
something you're not telling me, is there? Something that I should know?"

"Nothing." He gave her gloved hands, folded as
they were upon her lap, a reassuring pat.

They were seated across from one another in
Litchfield's landau. The roof was opened in the
center and folded back, and a coachman in smart
striped blue and gold livery handled the ribbons
as the vehicle descended the cobbled streets of Tilbury toward the village docks. Next to Eleanor
there was a large picnic hamper which she had
brought. She'd let Litchfield look inside to inspect
the contents—a cold collation of breasts of duckling, fresh berries and plums, a good Chesire
cheese, lemonade, and a sponge cake that she'd

baked herself despite the cook's grumblings that a lady had no place in a kitchen. Eleanor had even let Mr. Weare taste one of the strawberries. He, on the other hand, had been frustratingly mysterious when she'd inquired about the black boxes which he'd brought and were sitting on his seat. There was one on each side of him, and she was dying to know what they held.

"You must wait until we get to Tilbury," Litchfield had insisted from her first query, and no matter how she tried to change his mind, he wouldn't let her peek inside either of them. "Only when we reach Tilbury may you look."

"Not just a peek? A teeny tiny peek?"

"No. By the bye, Miss Carew, were you such an inquisitive, impatient little thing when you were small?" he teased. The unbidden image of a delightfully young Miss Carew crossed his mind's eye. Her eyes were aglow with expectation, and she was hopping about a festooned fir tree at Christmas, pretty as an angel with a heavy dark braid down her back, and begging her papa to let her open the biggest boxes first. She probably even squealed when she opened presents. No doubt rubies would send her over the moon, he mused. But he gave no hint of these thoughts. All he said was, "I imagine your parents must have spoiled you dreadfully, and now 'tis I who must pay the piper for their indulgence."

"My mother would have liked to spoil me. My father never cared," she replied without thinking.

That image of Miss Carew surrounded by brightly wrapped presents faded from Litchfield's mind. He tried not to frown. "Ah, yes. Well, that doesn't sound in the least bit agreeable, and since we're to have nothing but a good time—escape, I believe you termed it—I shan't ask you any more about that, except to tell you that it shall be my pleasure to spoil you this day."

The coach slowed to a stop, and the clip-clop of horses' hooves upon cobblestones was replaced by the cry of seabirds overhead. Eleanor looked at Mr. Weare, cocked an inquisitive brow, then eyed the black boxes.

"Not quite yet," he said. "You must learn patience, Miss Carew."

The coachman descended from the landau, unfolded the steps for Litchfield and Eleanor to alight, then took the wicker hamper from Eleanor's seat and headed away as if he knew where he was going.

"Now may I look?" Eleanor asked when they were alone, and she could no longer contain herself. "Oh, please."

"Yes, now you may," he said with his own measure of excitement as he set one of the boxes on her lap. Litchfield had never known there could be such pleasure in giving, but his urge to smile was dampened by a gnawing anxiety that Miss Carew might not appreciate what was inside. He waited and watched as she folded back the tissue to reveal a dome of black felt, a touch of gold braid, a panache of silver plumes.

"A hat?" she wondered aloud, then reached inside the box to pull it out and reveal a lady's bonnet styled like that of a pirate's hat. She laughed. It was that sweet musical sound Litchfield so relished, and to his astonishment, Miss Carew leaned across the space between their seats to give him a light kiss upon the cheek. Her voice rang with enthusiasm. "I love it. It couldn't be more perfect, Mr. Weare. Thank you. Whatever gave you such an idea? So clever and amusing. And thoughtful. How did you know I'd secretly been coveting pirate hats? Tell me, how do I look?" she asked, taking off the Oldenburg bonnet to set the pirate hat upon her head.

"It's perfect," Litchfield said, and he drank in

the delicious sight of her. She was wearing the most charming dress in royal blue cloth with a high waist and apron front laced like a peasant's bodice with colored ribbons of green and gold and blue. She'd never looked more like a Gypsy than she did in that dress with that pirate hat sitting at a jaunty angle atop those glossy black curls. Desire coiled within him, and his blue eyes burned with yearning as their gazes locked.

Damnation, man, kiss her, an inner voice urged Litchfield. *You'll never have a better moment than this.* But he didn't. He didn't budge, for he wasn't sure he wanted to kiss her just then. At least not in so public a setting where all the world might see. He still wanted Miss Carew more than any other woman, and he would have her. Images of Miss Carew lying against pure white sheets, those glossy black curls fanning out about her and her red lips waiting for his touch tormented him, yet he knew he'd made the right choice to wait, and a long loaded silence stretched between them.

"Have you one as well? A hat?" Eleanor was the first to speak, her tone a tad too merry, for she, too, had sensed the tension of desire and unfulfilled longing. Taking the lid off the other box, she pulled out a second hat. "Ah, there is one in here. Let me put it on you." And once done, she sat back to regard him. She smiled in satisfaction. "If there should be nothing more to this day beyond this morning, I would remember it always."

Litchfield's chest contracted. He nodded in silent acknowledgment. Miss Carew had the most uncanny ability to ruffle him with the simplest remarks. Thinking about what she'd said and about the kiss he hadn't taken, he spoke softly:

"You kissed me a moment ago."

Eleanor blushed and looked down at her hands.

"May I return the pleasure?" he asked in a low caressing whisper.

Her eyes grew wide and her heart began to beat
rapidly. She was thinking about velvet again. He
was making her entertain wanton thoughts about
kisses and taking risks, and she wondered, for an
instant, if it was truly such a wise idea to go on
this excursion with Mr. Weare.

He saw her confusion and was quick to clarify,
"I merely wanted to thank you for accepting my
gift with such an open mind."

And before she might say another word he
dropped a chaste kiss upon her cheek. Chaste
though it was, a kiss was still a kiss, and Eleanor
required several moments before she could look at
him again.

He gave a gentle cough. "Are you ready,
Madam Pirate, to board your vessel?"

"Aye, Captain, I am." He had put her at ease,
and she laughed.

Litchfield assisted Eleanor from the carriage, and slipped his arm through hers. Overhead, sea gulls circled and called to one another,
and as Litchfield and Eleanor walked the length of
the pier every ship carpenter, sailor, collier, and
warehouseman on the Tilbury docks stopped their
labor to stare.

"Faith, Mr. Weare, my new hat is getting a vast
amount of attention. Who knows, you may start
the latest fashion rage, and all the modistes shall
call them Tilbury bonnets."

"It's not the hat, Miss Carew. It's you beneath
it," Litchfield corrected, finding he was jealous
again. He wasn't accustomed to that, and he hur-
ried Miss Carew on board the *Windsong*. He didn't
want those rough men, some of them foreigners
and half-clad in the morning sun, staring at her.
Or more precisely, he didn't want them entertaining the sort of lustful thoughts of which he was
guilty.

"Shouldn't we bring someone else along for the

voyage, sir?" asked Eleanor as she regarded the *Windsong*. The yacht was larger than the flat barge upon which they had floated up the Thames. There was a towering mast, some sort of billowy front sail, and in the center deck, there was a shaded sitting area with colorful cushions and a low table upon which the coachman had set the picnic hamper.

"Don't tell me you're worried about being alone with me!" teased Litchfield.

"No, it's not that. It's the boat that worries me. It's an awfully lot larger than the other one we went out in."

"Nothing to worry about. I'm a fairly competent sailor. Learned to handle a tiller when I was still in knee breeches. Though I might need a bit of your help. Holding the sheet line, that sort of thing, y'know. Could you manage, if I needed it?"

"I suppose. You'll have to teach me, though, and you shall have to be patient."

"Teach you? Of course I shall. And if you take to the sea like you did to handling the ribbons of my phaeton, then I've nothing to fear."

They sailed out past Allhallows Point and into the mouth of the Thames. A steady wind was coming out of the northeast so they tacked northward up the coastline and into the archipelago around Wakering. Three hours had passed since leaving Tilbury when they dropped anchor in a cove to enjoy the luncheon Eleanor had brought. After dining, Litchfield fished while Eleanor, who had declined his invitation to be taught that particular skill, read a copy of Sir Walter Scott's latest work.

Eleanor glanced up from the book to regard the darkening sky. "It must be later than I thought."

"No, it's not late," Litchfield replied. Quickly, he reeled in an empty hook and set the fishing rod aside. "There's a storm approaching, I fear."

"Will we make it back in time?"

"There's no way." A roll of thunder confirmed this as he studied the eastern horizon that was getting darker by the second, then he glanced toward the west and the beachfront which was several hundred yards away. Looking back at the gathering storm, he watched the first streak of lightning break through the clouds. His tone became rather forbidding. "There won't even be enough time to make it to the shore."

Eleanor followed the direction of his gaze and saw the heavy line of thunderheads where the sea met the sky. They were positively ominous. Another roll of thunder rumbled closer, followed by more lightning. "Will we be all right, do you think?"

"There's sufficient shelter here in the cove. Much better, much safer than if we'd already started down the coast. We can be thankful for that. At least we'll be protected from the brunt of it, and if we drop the sails to ride out the storm, the worst we'll get is a thorough drenching. There'll be no helping that, I regret."

"It sounds an adventure. I used to love to play in the rain as a child," Eleanor said, sounding braver than she was, for she knew this storm wasn't the sort in which one played. Already the wind in the cove had picked up considerably, and she watched as Mr. Weare lowered the sails. There were whitecaps on the water, and the boat was bouncing about as if a giant's hand had swooped down to churn the water. Mr. Weare finished securing the sails none too soon and scurried beneath the scant protection of the awning that covered the sitting area toward the bow of the boat.

It was pitch black when the sky opened up, the blinding deluge accompanied by deafening cracks of thunder. Eleanor and Litchfield huddled together under the awning. He'd been right. They were quickly drenched, the force of the wind driving the rain beneath the striped canvas roof. She shivered, and he draped a picnic blanket across her shoulders, quite by accident knocking the pirate hat from her head. In the next instant, a gust of wind pulled it from Eleanor's lap and toward the back of the boat. She moved to retrieve it.

"No!" he hollered at her. "Don't go after it."

But Eleanor didn't hear him above the storm. She only knew that she didn't want to lose that hat, and without thinking she darted from beneath the awning.

Of a sudden, the wind shifted, the boat listed to one side, and the heavy boom swung toward Eleanor's back. Again Litchfield yelled a warning, and again she didn't hear. The boom hit Eleanor squarely in the shoulders, knocking her forward several feet to teeter at the edge of the boat, and she grabbed the nearest thing to prevent herself from falling overboard. Later, she was to learn that she'd grabbed, thereby untying, the rope that secured the sails. That was how the sails had loosened, been filled with rainwater and carried to the bottom of the cove. At the time, she only cared that there was something to stop her from pitching over the side, and, terrified by her narrow escape, aching from the thwack of the boom, she cowered in the rain, clutching that single lifeline until Mr. Weare appeared to guide her back beneath the awning.

At first, Litchfield wanted to rant at Miss Carew, to berate her for such extraordinary foolishness, but the dressing-down wouldn't come. All he could think was how close he'd been to losing her, to seeing her topple over the side of the *Windsong* and disappear forever beneath the stormy water. It was too hideous to consider, and instead of harsh words, he held her. He couldn't get out of his mind that moment when the boom had hit her and he'd thought she was going to pitch overboard. He held her closer, perhaps a bit too tightly as he smoothed sodden curls off her face. He didn't want to ever let her go.

Eleanor nestled in the security of his arms. She felt safe in Mr. Weare's embrace, and she sighed, hardly aware of the throbbing in her shoulders or the howl of the wind and the pounding of the rain and waves. She dozed off, the storm passed, and when Eleanor opened her eyes the first thing she saw was the tiny moon-shaped scar beneath Mr. Weare's eye.

"How did you get the scar?" she asked, feeling that somehow the storm had brought them closer and she could now ask such a personal question.

He'd hardly expected this. A grateful embrace, perhaps, but a question about his scar, no. Caught off guard, he blinked twice and wondered which tale to tell her. There was the runaway phaeton on the mall; he always claimed to have saved a young lad from certain death on that particular day. Or there was the band of thieving tinkers on Hounslow Heath. Perhaps the duel in Brighton would appeal to Miss Carew, or the wreck off Cowes during race week on the Isle of Wight when he'd rescued an American widow from the surf. One story was as good as the other. He never told the truth. That was far too painful.

"It was nothing more than a silly accident," he lied. "Truth to tell, it's rather embarrassing in hindsight. I fell from a hayloft as a lad."

"Oh," she said softly, one warm slender finger rising to touch the puckered ridge. "I was rather expecting something heroic."

He swallowed hard. Damnation, he should have gone with the runaway phaeton. Her reaction was making him remember, and remembering was far worse than desire, far worse than wanting her and not being able to have her. This was agony. She was bringing it back, all the sights and sounds, and the pain he'd buried deep inside. It was coming back, all the disillusionment, the heartbreak and self-loathing—for he, too, had thought he'd be a hero.

He'd only been twelve, not yet a man, and when he'd awakened to a room filled with smoke and the crackle of flames licking the embroidered draperies, he'd called out for his father in terror. It was only natural, everyone had assured him. After all, his father had loved him and kept him safe since his earliest memory. His father was strong and nothing, not even the fire, could hurt him, if his father was near. So he'd called to his father, and the earl had come to his son. Coughing, his face blackened, the cloth of his shirt seared, he'd rescued the boy and carried him to the rose garden, where father and son had stared at Litchfield Park. The house had been the Weare family seat since before Cromwell, and the boy had felt his father's suffering as they had watched the conflagration roar through the manor house, fire-red timbers splitting and falling, sparks flying against the night sky.

Somewhere inside the great house glass had shattered, and a woman had screamed, her cries high-pitched and thin with horror.

"Cecil! Sweet heaven, Cecil, where are you?"

They had heard her as if she were right beside them, but she wasn't.

"My God, it's your mother. Alicia, I'm coming," his father had called out, his voice sounding frightfully hoarse to the boy at his side, and when he'd tried to rise to go to his countess, the earl had collapsed on the pretty herringbone brickwork of the rose-garden path.

"Father." The boy had tried to rouse him; all the while his mother screaming from somewhere in the house. But the earl wouldn't move, and the boy had known what to do. He'd leapt to his feet, dashed down the herringbone walk and into the house. He had to rescue his mother.

The fire had been too strong, its heat so intense he'd felt its weight upon his lungs. He'd struggled for each breath as he made his way up the wide carved wooden staircase, past the two-storied stained-glass window toward the second floor where his mother's bedchamber faced the rose garden. With each step, the heat had become worse, the walls had become sheets of flames, and he'd only made it halfway to the landing before the stained glass window exploded and a shard of glass pierced his cheek. The boy had never made it to his mother. The staircase had groaned as if it might collapse beneath him, and he'd fled the house in fear.

Coward, the demons of his nightmares had accused him. His parents had given him everything, and he'd only taken from them. His father had perished saving him, and he'd failed to rescue his mother. He'd killed them. *Coward.* If it hadn't been for him, they would have survived. *Coward,* the demons had called, until he'd stopped feeling anything at all.

Eleanor touched his forearm, and Litchfield started, back to the present.

"You haven't heard a word I said. Where have you been these past few minutes? I didn't intend to upset you." There was a genuine edge of concern in her voice. "If I did, please forgive me."

"No. No, you didn't upset me. You mustn't worry. What were you saying?"

"There's someone on the shore over there. A farmer or fisherman, I believe. He's called out to us several times. He's realized we've lost our sails and wants to know if we need help."

Litchfield stood and cupped his hands to re-

spond to the farmer, and within minutes, arrangements had been made for a rowboat to come out
for them. Without its sails, the *Windsong* would remain in the cove while Eleanor and Litchfield returned to the metropolis by road, and an hour
later, having dried off in the farmer's cottage and
been served hot tea and buttered scones by the
farmer's wife, Eleanor and Litchfield climbed into
the back of the farmer's wagon to ride into town.

"Well now, Miss Carew, you must tell me truth-
fully, how did you like your adventure?"
Litchfield inquired as the sun set and the farmer's
cottage disappeared behind them. "Did you feel
like a pirate queen?"

"I'm sad to say, not a pirate queen. Rather more
like a drowned Bremen rat." Eleanor was having
the most dreadful time keeping her mind on the
conversation. Because there was no seat, nor even
a mattress on the wagon bed, and because of the
chill in the early evening air, Mr. Weare had insisted on taking her upon his lap. His arms were
wrapped about her waist, and his mouth when he
spoke seemed to brush against the nape of her
neck.

"Was it all that bad?" Litchfield, too, was highly
distracted. One of her breasts brushed against his
arm. Her slender legs slid across his thighs. She fit
against him quite well, too well, and he could
imagine all sorts of other ways they might fit together. The palm of one hand rested against her
thigh. It would be so easy to move that hand just
a few inches higher and into the valley her skirt
made at the top of her legs. Just a quick caress.
That was all he wanted. Nothing more. A quick
caress to satisfy himself that she was warm and
soft in that valley. His fingers flexed, and he allowed that hand to draw a pattern of little circles
on her skirt.

"I'm not so certain I'm cut out for adventure after all," she said in a throaty little voice. His hand was burning through her skirt where it went round and round, and she squirmed on his lap.

He swallowed hard. God, his hand was trembling, but there was little he could do in this open wagon with the farmer on the seat two paces away from them. She squirmed again, and he repressed a groan. He'd be a fool to give in to his desires when all she would remember was the cold wooden floor and the smell of wet hay. He essayed a light tone.

"Not cut out for adventure, you say. You disappoint me, Miss Carew. Does that mean you'd like to conquer the Marriage Mart and attain that perfect match after all?"

Eleanor thought of her mother and answered, "A perfect match? I don't know if there is such a thing. My parents had a hideous marriage."

Whatever remnants of his desire the farmer's proximity had failed to douse, the memories which had been jogged by her words completed. His desire was thoroughly dampened as he saw a picture of his mother seated before her easel in the rose garden at Litchfield Park. He couldn't think of his mother and seduction in the same breath, and he couldn't stop this memory any more than he could the last one.

"Addison, darling boy, do you think Father will like what Mummy's done?"

He'd studied the watercolor of his father dressed for the hunt, astride his gelding, a pack of hounds yapping at the horse's heels.

"Yes, ma'am. He'll be prodigiously pleased."

The painting was a welcome home gift from the countess to the earl, who had been visiting a family plantation in Jamaica for the past five months.

"Have you missed Father dreadfully?" the boy had asked his mother.

"Indeed, ever so much. My only solace has been

your company, my darling boy." She had given him a motherly embrace, then patted the empty spot on the marble bench for him to sit beside her.

"I think you and Father are special," he had said with an appropriate measure of childish awe. "You're not like other parents or other husbands and wives."

"Whatever do you mean, darling boy?" She had always looked directly at him when they conversed, always made him feel that he was someone special.

"Well, take George Randolph's parents. They have an *arrangement*." He had uttered this particular word as it if were some tropical oddity of nature.

"And what do you know of such things?"

"Only that Lord David is seldom home, and George doesn't get to sail or fish or hunt with his father. George says his mother is sad. Lady Mary cries a lot, he says."

Distress had crossed the countess's gentle face. She had not been a beautiful woman in the traditional sense, but her tender heart and kind nature had made her husband and son think she was the loveliest creature that had ever lived.

"That is very sad. For George and Lady Mary. And for Sir David, too, I should suppose, and I would cry, too, if I pondered such unpleasantries for too long." She had taken her son's hands in hers and gazed at his handsome features and into those blue eyes which were so like his father's. "You must promise me, darling boy, to find happiness. And love. I would not want you to be lonely like George and Lady Mary, and you must remember that where there is love one is never alone. You must never settle for less."

It had been many years since he'd thought of that conversation in the rose garden. For a long time he had wondered what it was his mother had

meant; then when he had thought that he understood the meaning of her words everything that
had been precious to him was gone, and he re-
fused to understand anymore. His mother had lied
to him. His adolescent heart was filled with anger
and doubt and self-hatred, for he had loved his
parents only to fail them and to be cast unrelent-
ingly alone into the world. Staring into the dark-
ness of the Essex countryside, he declared:

"I don't believe in love either."

Eleanor twisted about on his lap to peer at Mr.
Weare. She was puzzled. That wasn't what she'd
said. It wasn't what she'd meant, not at all, and
the vehemence of his remark rendered her speech-
less.

"Does that shock you, Miss Carew?" he asked.
There was a strident, almost mocking tone to this
question. He didn't sound like himself, but like
some cynical jaded roué. "You don't strike me as
the sort of young lady who falls in and out of
love."

She stiffened. "I'm not, Mr. Weare. But there are
many kinds of love, you know. Between friends,
for example. Or between a horse and his master.
Between a mother and child."

"You love your mother very much. You've mentioned her more than once. Perhaps you will tell
me about her one day." He was breaking all the
rules, but he didn't care anymore. Miss Carew was
causing him to develop some distinctly bad habits,
and he was rather glad.

"I do love her. I mean, I did. She's dead now."

Litchfield gazed down at Miss Carew's upturned face. He took in the bleak, helpless expression that caused the light in her eyes to fade, and
he watched as she blinked, tears spiking the ends
of her eyelashes.

"I've never seen you cry before," he said sol-
emnly.

"I'm not crying."

She swiped at the tears with the back of her hand. "When I was young I learned there's very little worth my tears. Crying certainly doesn't make things better."

He winced, for he knew what she was thinking. He'd felt her anguish. It had been his own, and he saw her sadness as if through a looking glass. He wanted to lessen the pain, to tell her he understood, but the words wouldn't come. It had been so long. He'd forgotten how to be honest with his feelings. The best he could think to say was:

"I'm sure you'll know that sort of love one day yourself. If you had such a love from your mother, the lady must have been special indeed, and if you follow in her footsteps, you'll be a wonderful mother yourself, giving a bounty of love and enjoying the reward of such love from your own children."

Something fluttered inside Eleanor's stomach. She had never considered her future in such a light, yet it was one of the most beautiful things anyone had ever said to her. So beautiful it made her heart ache with longing. It had nothing to do with freedom or adventure or independence of choice, but it was lovely to consider having a family of her own and experiencing that sort of love once again. It wasn't at all what she wanted, yet she couldn't help smiling as she leaned against his shoulder and closed her eyes.

And as the farm wagon rumbled across an open muddy field toward the Havering road, Eleanor's heart swelled with emotion. Eglantine would probably call it love, but Eleanor wasn't ready to speculate on that. It was trust that filled her heart, she reasoned. That's what it was. She trusted Mr. Weare. It was only natural since he had saved her twice now, and that could not help but forge a unique sense of connection. But more important to this swelling of emotion was the fact that he had been true to his promise. Eleanor wasn't a complete nodcock. She knew there had been more than one occasion when he could have taken advantage of her had he tried to do so, but he hadn't. He had pledged not to seduce her. He had promised to be a friend, and, indeed, that was what he had become.

Tomorrow, Eleanor decided, she would confide in Mr. Weare after their tea at The Bumblebee and Clover. It was the right thing to do. With the exception of Eglantine, who had the common sense of an empty pea pod, Mr. Weare was her only friend, the only other person in whom she might confide. Hopefully, once she had told Mr. Weare of her father's plans, Mr. Weare would be able to help her before she found herself in a situation from which she couldn't escape.

Eight

"**I**'LL HAVE A word with you, Miss High and Mighty!" The earl exploded into Eleanor's private chamber on the second floor of the Curzon Street town house.

It was barely ten o'clock the next morning, and Eleanor, who was still a bit tired from the storm and the uncomfortable ride home, was propped up in her bed with a tray of Belgian chocolate, fresh hot cross buns, and the latest issue of *La Belle Assemblée*. Her father had never entered her bedchamber before, and his unexpected presence so early in the day could only mean one thing. Something was amiss. Perhaps he had been informed of her late return last evening in a wrinkled and sodden state. Or perhaps some scheme was afoot. Had he drummed up another matrimonial prospect? Was there another Lord Gatcombe waiting downstairs to present himself to her? Eleanor set the fashion magazine aside.

"Yes, sir?" she inquired, affecting the manner of a dutiful daughter. If she didn't wish another unpleasant confrontation with her father, she knew it was necessary to appear as humble and obedient as possible.

The earl crossed to Eleanor's bed, but he didn't sit upon the nearby chair covered in emerald bro-

cade. Instead he hovered a few paces in front of
the canopied bed to stare at his daughter as if she
had sprouted the head of Medusa. Clearly, this
was not to be a pleasant interview.

"Saw Neddy Gatcombe. Wanted to have a word
with me and actually dragged me away from the
hazard table. Said it was important," the earl began, his choppy speech heavy with scorn. "Neddy
had some unexpected and most unpleasant intelligence to impart."

Eleanor didn't wither beneath this display of
contempt. In point of fact, it rather fortified her,
and she had to bite her tongue from retorting, *Everything about Lord Gatcombe is most unpleasant.* Instead, she replied, "I can't imagine what that
might be."

"I know *all* about *it*, you know. You didn't truly
believe you could deceive me with your little-
Miss-Innocent act, did you?"

For a heartbeat, Eleanor stared at her father,
struggling to hide her apprehension. Sweet
heaven, he did know about her outing yesterday?
It had been near midnight before she had arrived
home, and although her father had been out,
Eleanor suspected his valet probably reported this
intelligence to him. But what else did he know?
Did she know where she had been or with whom?
He couldn't be referring to Mr. Weare, could he?
Hoping that was not the case, Eleanor said nothing and waited for him to continue.

"It appears I was wrong to allow you so much
freedom. Thought you could be trusted, but you're
a sneaky one, aren't you! And don't look so wide-
eyed and innocent. I know your high and mighty
ways. Been slinking about behind my back,
haven't you? You've been seen entering some public house in Bloomsbury with a gentleman, you
know. Twice you've been seen. And you'll not
deny it."

Eleanor's stomach plummeted. He did know, but how much was the question. Her mind raced through the possibilities. Perhaps it was nothing more than that: she'd been seen. But who had seen her? And more importantly, had Mr. Weare been identified? Although not titled, he was a gentleman, and surely someone of the *ton* must know him. She'd never asked, but he might even be a member of White's or Boodle's. Oh, dear God, Eleanor hoped that was not the case, for she couldn't bear the certain humiliation if her father were to confront Mr. Weare. Somehow she managed to look the earl straight in the eye and maintain a steady voice. "I've done nothing of which to be ashamed."

"Hah! And a green gel like yourself would know about such things. A deceitful green gel, too, for I believed you were off ogling mummies and scarabs." He pointed an accusing finger at her. "You're a liar."

It was almost impossible for Eleanor to contain her temper. She counted to ten, then very slowly, very distinctly, she said, "I never lied to you."

"I didn't ask for your opinion. Mincing words, that's what you're doing. Well, you've made a fool of me, and you'll pay for this." The earl cut a brisk pattern between the canopied bed and the row of windows at the front of the bedchamber as if he were considering precisely how it was his high and mighty daughter would *pay* for this transgression. Facing her, he stabbed that accusing finger in the air above his head. "I've got my plans, you know that, and you'll not be interfering with them. Was that your intention? Did you mean to thwart me by ruining your reputation? It would be easy enough were you to become the latest nine-day wonder with a tumble in a scandal broth."

"That was not my intention." Eleanor sat tall in

defiance, and she was proud to say, "I was merely enjoying the company of a friend."

"Christ's nails, you're a fool, girl. A damned bloody fool. You've been listening to the Dowager Duchess of Exeter and her hoyden niece, no doubt. Everyone knows the old gel's mad as a hatter. *A friend*," he sneered, shaking his head in disbelief. "For once I'm going to give you some paternal advice, so you'd better listen well. There never was such a thing as friendship between a man and a woman, and the man's lying to you, if that's what you think is happening. A man's only got two things on his mind. First, there's what goes on behind closed doors with the weaker sex. After that it's his pockets. All men are either seducers or fortune hunters, and you'd be wise to accept that truth."

"No! That's not true, not at all." *Not my Mr. Weare. He would never consider such a thing. He made a promise to me,* her heart cried.

"I take it by that impassioned denunciation *your friend* hasn't yet seduced you. Well, thank God for small favors," the earl drawled in derision. "And he won't get the chance either, because as of this minute you're to be confined to your room until I decide what to do with you."

Confined to your room. The words echoed in her ears, making her think of her mother exiled at Mulgrave Manor. *Confined to your room.* The prospect was horrible. Unthinkable. Perhaps, she hoped, it was nothing more than a threat, and she could appease him.

"Please, sir, don't confine me to my room. That's not necessary." Visions of Lady Penelope, patient and ever hopeful, waiting for a brighter day that never came, flashed across Eleanor's mind's eye. To be treated in this way by the man who had destroyed her mother was a fate too horrible to consider, and Eleanor could not keep the mounting desperation from her voice. "I'll do as you say, I promise,"

"You'll do as I say? And a poor wager that would be," the earl scoffed. "I seem to recall a similar promise once before. Believe me, this time, my dear Miss High and Mighty, you'll be doing just that—doing as I say—because this time I'm going to guarantee it."

The earl turned on his heel and quit Eleanor's room, giving the door an angry slam behind him. A funny hollow silence surrounded her as the thud faded away, then she heard something. From the corridor came the distinct sound of a key turning and a bolt falling into place.

"No!" She jumped up from the bed and rushed across the room to try the door. But the handle wouldn't turn. "You can't do this!"

"I can and I did. And I'll be back for you when it's time," the earl pronounced with cool finality. There was the most irritating note of triumph in his voice. "In the meanwhile, I wouldn't waste any energy trying to get out of there. It won't do you any good. The staff is under strict orders not to let you leave the house. It's for your own good, m'dear," he ended with a laugh. "For your own good. I'm your father and I do know what's best."

Once again, Eleanor bit back a reply. She wanted to scream in defiance of him, but she would never let him know how much he had upset her, and, struggling to maintain her calm, Eleanor went back to the bed and sat down to consider her predicament. It wasn't going to be all that bad, she told herself. Even if she missed her afternoon meeting with Mr. Weare at Montague House, she was certain to be out before the next day. She and her father were scheduled to attend Lord and Lady Carisbrooke's turtle dinner at eight this evening, and Eleanor suspected that tonight someone would return to unlock the door and by seven-thirty her father would be escorting her to the affair. He'd already gloated that several of his chums, who were widowers and dangling about for young wives, would be in attendance. He was banking on generating interest in his daughter at this particular affair, and Eleanor was certain she would be released in order to be paraded about the Carisbrooke receiving rooms.

At six-thirty, her suspicion was confirmed when a footman opened the door, and Eleanor's abigail entered.

"Where is the gown I selected for this evening?" inquired Eleanor, who was combing her hair at the dressing table. It was later than when she usually began her toilette, and she would have to hurry to be ready within the hour. "Had you forgotten that my amethyst silk gown needed to be pressed? Isn't it ready?"

" 'Fraid I can't be saying, my lady." Young Jilly bobbed a curtsy as she set a tray on the tea table in front of the hearth. Jilly wasn't really an abigail, having only been elevated from scullery maid upon Eleanor's arrival, and she was eager to please her mistress.

Eleanor set her silver brush aside and eyed the tray. "What's that for?"

"Dinner, my lady. Glazed partridge and your favorite pudding." Jilly bobbed another wholly unnecessary curtsy and forced a thin smile. Something was awry in the Curzon Street town house. The earl was in a foul humor, the footmen were tiptoeing about as if the floors were littered with eggshells, and Jilly hoped that her career as a lady's maid was not in jeopardy.

"Dinner? Whatever for? My father and I are going out for dinner this evening."

A bright red flush crept up Jilly's forehead and beneath the ruffle of her white cotton mobcap. "Beg pardon, my lady, but his lordship instructed me to tell you he canceled the plans. His lordship sent Joseph, the third footman, round to Lady Carisbrooke's with a note. His lordship told me you were ailing, my lady, but you don't look under the weather. Not atall." She peered at her mistress. Perhaps it was that time of the month, but she dared not ask, for *ladies*, young Jilly had discovered, never discussed such things. "Are you *all right?*" she inquired, putting a peculiar emphasis on the query in the hopes that Lady Eleanor would understand.

"No, I'm not all right," Eleanor confessed, possessing not the vaguest notion what Jilly meant. Her thoughts were focused on her father and the future. She had misjudged the depth of her father's anger, and Eleanor found herself at a loss to second-guess what he might do next. She'd thought she understood him, but she was wrong, foolishly so. Clearly, she had lingered too long in his household, and it was time, she concluded, to proceed with her earlier plan to disappear into the greater metropolis and establish a life of her own. It had been a nice idea to imagine that she could confide in Mr. Weare and rely upon his assistance, but that's all it had been. A nice idea. This was, as it had always been, something Eleanor was going to have to do on her own. As soon as she was released from this room, she would be gone from her father forever.

"Would you like a hot compress, my lady?" Jilly mistook the expression of deep concentration upon Eleanor's face for discomfort. "My mum always likes one at these times of the month."

"That's not what I meant, Jilly." In spite of herself, Eleanor smiled. "It's not my health but my temperament that's out of sorts. It's my father, you see. We had a bit of a disagreement."

"I understand, my lady. I saw him." There was

an almost conspiratorial note to Jilly's sympathetic reply.

"He was tremendously angry?"

Jilly nodded. "Tremendously," she parroted Lady Eleanor, after whom she had decided to model herself.

"So I'm to remain in my room tonight." Eleanor was stoic. It wasn't hard to be resigned to her immediate fate. She'd endured eighteen years at the mercy of her father's whims; a few more days wouldn't matter. "Of course, it shall only be until the morning, when my father will hopefully have forgotten what it was that angered him in the first place. Well, I suppose one night isn't too much to bear. Is it? Will you stay and keep me company, Jilly?"

"Oh, yes, my lady," was the abigail's eager reply. Lady Eleanor had been teaching her to read the captions on the fashion illustrations, and she liked that immensely.

In the morning, however, nothing had changed. There were no instructions from the earl to unlock the door, which a footman continued to guard, letting only Jilly in and out with meal trays. And thus was the pattern for the next few days. Eleanor was not permitted to leave her room, nor receive visits from Eglantine or the dowager duchess. Her only companion was Jilly, and she passed the time writing in her journal, reading, or sitting at the window seat to watch the pedestrian and carriage traffic on Curzon Street. Each day when the sun set, a measure of her initial tolerance and hopefulness eroded. By the fifth day, her optimism was virtually gone, and Eleanor did something rash.

She was reading a book in the window seat above Curzon Street when a coach bearing the Exeter coat of arms stopped before the town house. Whether the dowager duchess or Eglantine was in the carriage Eleanor could not tell, and she knelt upon the window seat to press her nose against the glass and watch as the coachman climbed down from the driving box to mount the town house steps.

A few minutes passed before the coachman returned to the carriage. He paused at the open carriage window. There was a passenger inside, for he was clearly conveying a message to someone, and Eleanor did not hesitate to fling wide her window and call out:

"Up here. Eglantine! Your grace? Is that you? It's me, Eleanor. I'm up here."

But whoever was in the carriage didn't hear. Nor did the coachman, who climbed back onto his box and picked up the ribbons to wheel the vehicle away from the curb. The carriage window closed, and Eleanor watched the coach roll down Curzon Street until she could see it no longer.

"Hello down there!" she called to the flower girl on the corner, but the wind carried her cries away.

Her cries had, however, echoed through the town house. The earl had heard them and was livid. Within the hour, Eleanor was escorted to a small sparsely furnished room on the third floor. It was a room with only one window, a window which did not face Curzon Street, and if Eleanor called out, only the doves beneath the eaves would be disturbed.

The day was waning, the light was fading fast, long shadows crept up the yellowing walls, and the small room with a frayed counterpane seemed unbearably dreary. For the first time, Eleanor was frightened. Her final vestiges of hope vanished, loneliness settled about her with an actual physical sensation, and for the first time, she thought of Mr. Weare with unbearable longing. It was a startling thing to accept that somehow he had become important to her, so important that she began to worry more about what Mr. Weare was thinking and doing than about how she would escape her father's household. For the first time, she realized it wasn't the prospect of freedom, but her friendship with Mr. Weare that was threatened by her father and this confinement.

What was Mr. Weare doing? she wondered. She thought of his kisses and his smiles, the lovely low tremor in his deep voice and the penetrating gaze in his blue eyes, and her heart ached at the thought that some other young lady might be enjoying them. That some other young lady might be sailing with him or driving through the countryside on a sunny afternoon was a miserable possibility to consider. The most discomposing image of some unknown female wearing a pirate hat from Mr. Weare deepened Eleanor's misery, and she sniffled, wishing that she had been able to save her hat; then, at least, she would have that small momento to which she might hold.

Did he even care that she had disappeared? Surely he must have wondered why she hadn't appeared at the museum at the appointed hour on that afternoon following their sailing outing. Had he perhaps made queries about her? Perhaps searched for her coachman? He might find her that way. Or had he given her up? Oh, that she might find him and explain what had happened. But perhaps that might never happen. Perhaps her father would triumph over her, and she would never see Mr. Weare again.

With a sinking sensation, Eleanor realized she was truly her father's prisoner, and that was when she broke down and cried.

Nine

I T WAS AN unremarkable Friday evening at Madame Fournelle's. Pale clouds of smoke wafted onto Lisle Street as a footman opened the front door of the notorious hell to admit the Earl of Litchfield. Inside the marble vestibule the sharp scent of Virginia tobacco mingled with exotic perfumes from Persia and India. Litchfield inhaled. The hint of a smile touched his lips, and for a moment, he paused to appreciate the familiar sounds that greeted him. From upstairs, there came the invitation of light female laughter and the tinkling of crystal wine glasses, and from the series of connecting saloons on the ground floor, he heard the irresistible music of coins being raked by a croupier. It was good to be back.

Although not yet midnight, the Frenchwoman's establishment was crowded cheek-to-jowl. Madame's girls, rouged and coiffed, their thin muslin gowns dampened, mingled with the usual assortment of gamesters, gentlemen for whom—having been blackballed by one or more of Mayfair's fashionable clubs—Madame Nicolette Fournelle's was the only avenue through which to indulge their fondness for the green baize. Or, at least, it was the only venue in which one might forfeit a king's ransom ensconced in the requisite trappings of comfort and style that included the finest French brandy and an enticing variety of cyprians.

In the magenta saloon, an opulent room with moiré walls and pastel cherubim upon the ceiling, the tables were dedicated to hazard, and it was there, every Friday, that the high-flying lordlings Eaton, Hammond, and Westbridge could be found. They were Rugby men, the three having been roommates at the prestigious school, and sadly, each gentleman's estate was mortgaged to the hilt. Being perpetually under the hatches, even the family jewels had been pawned. Yet nothing would stop the friends from playing for staggeringly steep stakes, and before the night was over, they would sign chits with the gullgropers hovering in Madame Fournelle's Jerusalem Chamber. Addicted to the roll of the dice, there was only one other pastime more crucial to their well-being, and that was the eternal hunt for the hand of an heiress. Hence their moniker *Les Monsieurs Chasseurs*. The hunters had not, however, met with good fortune on that front either.

Beyond the cherubs and magenta moiré, the gold saloon was devoted to even-odd. Illegal since 1745, E.O. remained as wildly popular as ever. It was the particular vice of the Marquis of Lambe and of Sir Reginald Skeffington, an aged roué and defrocked cleric. There was a third habitué of Madame Fournelle's who gravitated to the gold saloon: Lord Fortune, the Earl of Litchfield, for whom the seat opposite the wheel was reserved out of deference for his high stakes, limitless pockets, and unceasing luck. *On dit* Litchfield brought good fortune to those nearest him, and on occasion, the luckless Lambe and the elderly Skeffington had been heard to squabble over who might sit beside him.

On this particular Friday night, Litchfield strutted into the gold saloon and took up his place at the head of the E.O. table.

"Evening, Fortune. Haven't seen you in a dog's age," quipped Skeffington as he scurried round the table to nab the seat to Litchfield's right.

The earl replied with a civil nod. He was in no mood for idle chatter.

"Been in the country, have you? Estate business, no doubt. Always a dreadful bore, don't you agree?" This came from Lambe as he inched his rotund figure into the space between Litchfield's and Skeffington's leather chairs. The Marquis of Lambe had suffered heavy losses the past four nights, and he was eager for a change of fortune. He delivered Skeffington a jab with his elbow. "Excuse me, sir, didn't know this seat was taken." But Skeffington made no effort to move, and Lambe again addressed Litchfield. "Sorry not to have had the pleasure of your company these past four nights. Most regretful. Most regretful, indeed. By the bye, sir, how are things in Hampshire?"

"Fine, Lambe," replied the earl. Of course, he hadn't been in the country on estate business, but he didn't bother to correct the old fellow. What was he to say? That he'd been closeted in his town house on Langham Place, stewing over the disappearance of some female? Who would believe anything so preposterous? Lord Fortune did not concern himself with such sensibilities. If the young woman in question did not wish to enjoy his company, then damn her. Why should he worry himself with what had happened to her? It was no concern of his.

"Bets, please," intoned the liveried croupier. He used his rake to indicate the stenciled E's and O's upon the felt-topped table.

Litchfield set fifteen crowns in a neat stack upon an E. Four other gentlemen placed their bets, the croupier spun the wheel and let the little ball drop. A waiter walked by with refreshments. Litchfield helped himself to a glass of champagne, and as the brass ball skittered and danced, popping in and out of the slots upon the wheel, he downed the beverage as if it were water. A sennight had elapsed since he'd last seen Miss Carew, during which time he had replayed the events of that day and evening in every fine detail, searching for some clue as to what he must have done wrong. Miss Carew had disappeared without a trace, she had failed to show up for their engagement the next day, and the highly unpleasant novelty of this rejection had yet to abate.

At first, Litchfield had assumed it was nothing more than a misunderstanding. Perhaps she'd developed a bit of a cold owing to the drenching storm and the chilly wagon ride. There were any number of reasonable explanations. For three days he had returned to Montague House, but there was no trace of Miss Carew or her coachman, and Litchfield was forced to conclude that he'd made a profound mistake. Miss Carew had not been worth the lofty promises. He'd been a fool to reveal so much of himself and an even greater fool to have acted with such sensitivity toward her. Such *restraint*. He should have seduced Miss Carew that first day—then at least he wouldn't be plagued by this lingering and wholly unsettling sensation as if there were unfinished business between them. He was getting softhearted, and it was bloody irksome.

The tiny brass ball was silent. Six pairs of eyes focused upon the wheel as it slowed to a stop.

"Odd!" the croupier declared.

Skeffington let out a whoop of delight. He'd won at last. So had Lambe.

Litchfield swore, but not at his loss. What did he really care about a fistful of crowns? It was Miss Carew who was the cause of his profanity, and verily, his anger had nothing to do with *unfinished business*; rather it was the fact that he missed Miss Carew. How could he have let such a thing happen? How could he have allowed himself to become attached to anyone? How could he have let the memories return? He knew better than that. He'd learned his lesson years ago the hard way, and he'd done an admirable job of controlling himself. Until Miss Carew.

"Bets, gentlemen." The croupier was about to spin the wheel once again.

Litchfield set another stack of crowns on the table and helped himself to a second flute of champagne, which he downed as swiftly as the first. Again the brass ball dropped and skittered, the wheel stopped, and this time, Litchfield had won, but so focused were his thoughts upon Miss Carew that he hardly heard the tinkle of coins as the croupier raked them across the felt.

He missed her. This was a staggering acknowledgment, and of course, it wasn't something he liked to admit, having worked hard to stay away from any sort of attachments. But the truth of the matter was for the first time since his parents' death sixteen years ago he'd allowed himself to become attached to something. He hadn't even realized how important spending those afternoons with Miss Carew had become, and he was angry at himself for being so weak as to have let that happen. Lord Fortune didn't need anyone.

He nabbed another glass of champagne and peered over the crystal rim at madame's girls. Although he didn't need anyone, he did need female distraction. There was the Highland redhead named Kat lounging on a velvet settee and the sweet Eliza was standing by the door; and he chuckled, remembering the passionate interludes he'd shared with each of these barques of frailty, but his regard didn't linger upon either of these former companions. His gaze moved on, circling the room, subconsciously searching for a black-haired Gypsy beauty with deep-red lips and flashing golden brown eyes.

A ruckus in the magenta saloon drew Litchfield's attention from the futile search. The voices of the Rugby lordlings were raised in a fever pitch of excitement.

"What's that?" wondered Lambe, who never liked to think that he might be missing something.

"*Les Monsieurs Chasseurs*," was Skeffington's dry reply, a note of jealousy rising in his voice. "Do you suppose the lads are enjoying a streak of good luck?"

All occupants of the gold saloon looked toward the arched doorway as Lord Boulton, another Rugby man, crossed the threshold and burst into speech:

"We're off to Mulgrave's. Open invite to one and all." Boulton's face was flushed. He, too, was in the grips of some sort of frenzy.

"What's the occasion?" Lambe was already on his feet. It didn't really matter what the occasion might be. Whatever it was, if it was generating this much excitement, he was going to be part of it.

Boulton explained, "Seems Mulgrave fell into serious debt to Captain Whimper."

"Whimper, you say," Skeffington uttered the blackleg's name with a touch of dread. Having mastered the arts of fraudulent card play, Captain Whimper ranked among London's most notorious swindlers who claimed gambling as their profession. A man of dubious birth, Whimper was also known as a man of perverse appetites and as a deadly duelist. Skeffington shook his head in sympathy. "Poor Mulgrave. But what does this have to do with an invitation to his town house?"

"He's proposed an all night loo game to honor

his vowel to Whimper, and you'll never guess what he's wagered."

"The keys to his wine cellar?"

"A case of Irish whiskey?" Everyone knew that next to his French brandy, Mulgrave's hoard of whiskey was his most prized possession.

"Hardly. This is rather more serious than spirits," drawled Boulton, who paused a moment to heighten the impact of his revelation. "He's staked his daughter."

"The devil you say!" The eager Lambe froze in his tracks. He could hardly credit such a diabolical thing, and he raised a quizzing glass through which to regard Boulton.

"It sounds precisely what I'd expect of Vile Villiers," remarked the defrocked Skeffington. He grinned. "Rather a tantalizing proposition, wagering one's own daughter. Although I didn't know Mulgrave had any offspring."

"Only one." Boulton, who owned a fondness for gossip, was a font of intelligence this evening. "Been hidden away at one of his smaller estates. On the Berkshire downs, I believe."

"Sounds hideously dreary."

"Why'd he bring her to Town?"

"His countess died."

"Ah, I had heard something about that. An unobliging wife. Arctic, Mulgrave claimed."

"Yes, well, the lady finally departed this world, leaving the girl, and Mulgrave brought her to town a few weeks ago. She just turned nineteen."

"In town for the Season and no offers yet?" slurred a foxed gentleman who had wandered into the gold saloon. "Not hard on the eye, is she?"

"Quite to the contrary. Lady Eleanor's a tasty bit of baggage," Boulton asserted. "Saw her once myself. Riding on Rotton Row with the Duchess of Exeter's great-niece."

"Heard the chit's a bit of a hoyden," remarked

another newcomer, Lord Claremont. The clutch of gentlemen gathered about the E.O. table had multiplied, and they were all ears for this juicy morsel of tattle. Being themselves black sheep, it was distinctly elevating for their collective morale when gossip featured someone other than themselves.

"A hoyden? Who?" This from Lambe again. "Do you mean Lady Eleanor or the dowager duchess's great-niece?"

"The pair," ventured Claremont, who raised his hands in mock alarm. "A pair of hoydens!"

"Hoydens, you say. And when did that ever bother you, Claremont? Thought you liked 'em frisky," Skeffington jested. Ribald laughter rippled through the room.

"The chit needs a man to put her in line, eh?" a fellow called from the edge of the crowd. "Do you suppose Whimper is up to the task?"

"If he wins," Boulton said with a shrug.

"So we're all to come and witness the spectacle," Litchfield, who had been following this conversation, remarked in derision. He'd never liked Mulgrave. The earl didn't know how to control his excesses, nor did he have the least bit of charm. Litchfield frowned. He could tolerate just about anyone, *if* they had an ounce of charm. Even Whimper possessed his own sort of charm.

"Even better. We're not invited to be mere witnesses, but participants." Boulton leered. "The game is open to anyone who wishes to sit at the table and try for a chance at the pool as well as the gel."

A round of low whistles rippled through the gold saloon. The prospect of staking one's fortune and luck against the likes of Captain Whimper was a distinctly unfavorable proposition, but the temptation of a daughter just out of the schoolroom made it priceless and quite compelling. What red-blooded gamester could turn his back on such a wager? No wonder the gentlemen were abuzz.

Skeffington rose from the E.O. table to follow Lambe and the others. The notion of winning a comely young female was intoxicating. Like all the gentlemen at Madame Fournelle's he loved a good bet, the steeper the better, and despite the shadow of Captain Whimper, this was an irresistible temptation.

"How about you, Fortune? Are you game?"

"Don't see why not." Litchfield pocketed his winnings, grabbed a bottle of champagne from a waiter, and followed the bosky crowd onto Lisle Street.

The noise level in Mulgrave's vestibule was deafening. The neo-Classical rotunda, designed by one of the venerable Adam's protegés, presented the ideal setting for bejeweled matrons and blushing ingenues, not for the raucous crowd waiting to ogle the girl. The gathering of gamesters—and their bawdy remarks—was in stark contrast to the elegant and tasteful setting. The exquisite tile floor had been executed in rich reds and blue-greys, the ceiling were ornamented with delicate blue plasterwork, and the semicircular perimeter of the rotunda featured splendid columns of marble. Litchfield leaned against one of those columns, raised the bottle of champagne to his lips and watched the goings-on.

There wasn't a sober soul among the lot, Litchfield included. A retinue of footmen had been passing out samples from Mulgrave's coveted hoard. It was an old trick: encourage the challengers to over imbibe; it evened the odds in the host's favor. Skeffington looked as if he might pass out on the tiled floor by the time Mulgrave appeared at the top of the curving marble staircase. A young lady, her head hanging so low as to hide her face, was at his side.

"Prime article, Mulgrave." This remark came from one of the Rugby lordlings and was followed by several other comments, some quite explicit, for the young lady was dressed in a dampened gown that outlined pert breasts, a tiny waist and the hint of shapely legs. The bodice had been pulled low on the shoulders to reveal an expanse of soft creamy skin, and, in contrast, dark curls, loosened as if in preparation for the privacy of her boudoir, tumbled over one shoulder.

"Most unsporting of you, Mulgrave, to have kept her hidden away for so long," quipped Boulton.

"Didn't I see the wench strutting down the path in Vauxhall?" Lord Claremont called out.

"Sure she's your daughter?"

"Indeed, sirrah, she is my daughter! But not for long." Mulgrave chuckled. "Gentlemen, allow me to present my daughter, Lady Eleanor Villiers. Take a good look, sirs, for one of you shall claim her before the next sun rises."

Lady Eleanor did not lift her head, yet her fear and loathing were palpable, and Litchfield experienced a jolt of repugnance. He shouldn't have come here. This wasn't amusing; it was revolting. And riveting. In spite of himself, Litchfield couldn't take his eyes off the girl Mulgrave held tightly with one arm and forced to descend the staircase by his side.

Halfway down the sweep of marble stairs, Mulgrave paused to whisper something in his daughter's ear. It was evident by the tension in his facial muscles that whatever the earl had said was not pleasant. When Lady Eleanor didn't respond, he gave her a quick little threatening shake, and this time, the young woman looked up.

Her poise was breathtaking. Although Lady

Eleanor wasn't tall, she stood as straight as some mythical warrior queen. She seemed to tower over Vile Villiers, and there was pride, nay, defiance in the tilt of her head. She didn't flinch as she returned the crowd's stare, and when she looked toward Litchfield's corner he felt as if he'd been punched in the chest, for he imagined he recognized Mulgrave's lovely daughter. He'd had too much to drink, and he set the champagne bottle in a statuary alcove, then rubbed a shaking hand across his eyes before taking a second look.

This time his reaction was more violent. His chest contracted and the air seemed to be sucked from his lungs. He hadn't been mistaken. The young lady to be staked in loo this night was his innocent Miss Carew, and for one crazy moment, Litchfield almost crossed the vestibule to snatch her away from Mulgrave and remove her from the town house. But he held back, an onset of unfamiliar emotions racing through him like a waterspout across a calm sea.

First, there was comprehension, followed by an unfamiliar rush of compassion, and then shame. He was no better than anyone else in this room. They were, the lot of them, no better than a pack of wild beasts, and for the first time in years, Litchfield experienced the sting of remorse, along with a moment's wish that he might disappear into the fancy blue plasterwork before she saw him among them and knew the kind of man he truly was. He hadn't been jilted or slighted by Miss Carew, yet in his infinite selfishness he'd had no thoughts save those for his own immediate gratification and his wounded male pride. The reason why she had vanished became clear, as did the meaning behind those wistful references to home and her parents.

It makes me very happy, sir, to be able to spend these afternoons in your company.

At the time, Litchfield had assumed her words were nothing more than flirtation. Now he knew otherwise. It was an ugly twist of irony that he— Lord Fortune, rogue and womanizer—had been her retreat from Vile Villiers.

Rescue me. Take me to that pirate ship and sail to the farthest corner of the earth.

How well she had hidden her desperation. Living in this household had to be nothing short of hell, Litchfield thought as Mulgrave began to explain the rules of play.

Litchfield didn't hear the specifics as he pushed away from the marble column to make his way toward the gaming table. Tomorrow would be soon enough to decipher his motivations.

Tonight there was only one course of action for Lord Fortune. He would enter the game, and he must win.

Ten

THE EARL OF Mulgrave was enjoying himself as he stood before the crowd to outline the rules of play. It wasn't often that he found himself in control of a situation, and having the rapt attention of every gentleman in the vestibule pleased him immensely. It was rather like holding court, he thought with an absurd note of self-flattery, and he emitted a series of satisfied chuckles between sentences. Everything was going as anticipated. A sizable crowd had made its way to his residence, a respectable number of whom were willing to play no matter what the terms, and Captain Whimper was most appreciative of the spectacle.

As was the earl's prerogative, he'd chosen five card loo with Jack of Clubs high, and he set the loo at an astronomical one hundred pounds, requiring players who failed to take a trick to pay a forfeit in that amount into the pool. The number of hands to be played was not specified, nor would there be a time limit on the play. It would be a round of elimination. All players would remain at the table until they were cleaned out. No debts could be voweled, all loos would be cash only, which elicited a few dissatisfied grumbles, for with such high stakes there were few men who carried that sort of blunt in their pockets. The final player remaining would win the pool—which, with a circle of six players, promised to be a small fortune—as well as the girl.

Seated a few paces away from the table, Eleanor heard every word of this. What her father described was medieval. It put her in mind of knights in a fight to the death, but Eleanor didn't think of herself as a fair maiden whose honor was being defended. Instead she felt like some cheap bit of chattel to be sold to the highest bidder.

It was only a few hours ago that her father had pounded on the door of the little room on the third floor under the eaves. "The time's come, Miss High and Mighty," the earl had called out as he'd unlocked the door and entered to dump a large dressmaker's box upon the bed.

Eleanor had glanced from her father to the dressmaker's box to the open door and then back to her father, not quite perceiving what was about to unfold. It had been approaching ten o'clock. She had been sitting at a makeshift writing table, composing her nightly journal entry, and she'd set the leather-bound notebook aside as a renewed flutter of hope lightened her heart. Perhaps this was the moment she'd almost lost all faith of ever seeing come to pass. Perhaps everything was about to return to the way it had been when she had first arrived in London. How she missed those carefree days and the round of activities, and how glad she would be to enjoy them once again.

Truth to tell, there was something else for which she would be glad, for it wasn't the rides in the park, nor the shopping with Eglantine, or even the freedom to do as she wished that had come to matter the most. All of that paled in comparison to the way her heart twinged each time she thought of Mr. Weare. Above all else it was Mr. Weare she missed. Oh, how she longed for the cozy chats they'd shared at The Bumblebee and Clover. How she ached to hear the rumble of his laughter as well as that low teasing voice, how she longed to engage once again in lively repartee.

Perhaps her father's appearance meant his anger had abated. Perhaps she was soon to be freed, and for one glorious moment, only the best seemed possible. But the earl's next words snuffed out those hopes as quickly as they had surfaced.

"I'm to be rid of you this night," the earl had said, this awful declaration ending in a triumphant grin. "Knew you'd be money in the bank, but I never dreamt it would be so quick and easy."

The meaning of her father's words had been clear to Eleanor. Dread had filled her. She had gone numb, the quill between her fingers had dropping to the table. "You've decided upon a husband for me?"

"In a manner of speaking." The earl had laughed.

"And who is the gentleman, if I may ask?" Eleanor's voice had trembled with apprehension.

"You may ask, but, truth is, I can't say precisely," had been his enigmatic reply.

Recalling her father's earlier threat to sell her to the Gypsies, Eleanor had been gripped by panic at the thought that he had embarked upon something unthinkable. With every shred of courage she could muster, Eleanor had inquired, "Would you care to explain yourself, sir?"

"No harm in it." That dreadful smile of triumph hadn't faded from his countenance. "You see, I found myself in a spot of trouble early this morning. Frightfully heavy debt to a scurrilous fellow, goes by the name of Captain Whimper, and after some consideration I came up with a way to appease the good captain. I'm hosting a gathering this evening. A little night of gaming to be precise."

"I fail to see what this has to do with me."

Eleanor had put on a brave front, although she had suspected he had affianced her to this captain in payment for his debt.

"Why, my dear, how could you say such a thing? It has everything to do with you. I was cleaned out last night, you see, with the exception of one asset. It's you, Miss High and Mighty. You're that asset, and tonight, I shall stake you to absolve my debt. Oh, what a glorious evening this shall be, for no matter what the outcome of the game, I'll come out ahead. Captain Whimper is so amused with the offer, my debt's been wiped clear, and if I win at loo, I'm plump in the pockets again. If I lose, well, at least I'm rid of you and my debt to Whimper in one clean sweep."

Eleanor could only stare at her father in horror. Sweet heaven, had she understood him? Her father was wagering her in a game of chance. Surely she couldn't have heard correctly. After this confinement, she had thought marriage to a stranger was the worst that might befall her, but this was beyond even that. The prospect of what this meant to her future was as horrifying as it was disgraceful, and her terror had been replaced by a flush of hot shame upon her cheeks as she'd struggled to prevent hysteria from rising in her voice. She had lashed out, "You can't do such a thing! It's immoral. Reprehensible. It's unnatural. And don't think for one moment that—"

"That you won't let me? That I can't get away with this?" he had snarled, and in his temper, a menacing carmine hue had sprouted upon his brow. His mean features had puckered together. "Listen *very* carefully, because I don't intend there to be any misunderstanding about what I expect from you tonight. I'm in serious debt to a man who'd sooner take my life than see me honor that debt, and though I suspect you couldn't care one way or the other on that account, I'm not ready to

face Saint Peter. I did warn you why I was bringing you to Town, and now it's time to play it
through. There's a gown in the box. You're to have
your abigail dress you and be ready within the
hour. You'll go downstairs with me, meet my
guests, and do as I say. Unnatural? Reprehensible?" He had given a blasé shrug. "No doubt it's
both. But it's perfectly legal, I assure you. A father's right, y'know, and whatever the outcome
this night you're to be naught but a respectful,
obedient daughter."

The earl had quit the room, making certain, of
course, to lock the door behind him, and Eleanor
had remained at the writing table staring at the
last words she had entered in her journal. *Tomorrow is another day*. That sentence had been written
under the assumption that sooner or later things
would return to the way they had been upon her
arrival in London, that soon her father's anger
would die down and he would release from this
room to parade her once again on the marriage
mart.

Gazing at that entry, Eleanor had been furious
with herself. How could she have been so naive?
Nothing was ever going to be the same, and it was
her fault. She'd wanted to be in charge, yet she'd
made nothing but wrong choices. What a hypo-
crite she'd been to have claimed that she wouldn't
tolerate an arranged marriage as long as she had
remained in her father's household, thereby accepting his authority over her. She never should
have stayed so long. She never should have allowed herself to enjoy Mr. Weare's company to the
point that she lost sight of why it was she had accompanied her father to town. It had only been a
means to an end, and yet how easily she had lost
sight of that end. She'd made a very wrong choice
indeed. Seething at her own stupidity, Eleanor had
slammed the journal closed, then she had set her

elbows on the table and propped her chin on her hands to consider what she must do. There was no time to spare and whatever it was, she must do it this night.

It had been in this meditative pose that Jilly had found Eleanor when she entered some time later.

"Oh, my lady, I've never seen his lordship like this before. Heard him humming a tune, I did. Most peculiar," the young abigail had bubbled with excitement. "Never seen him so pleased with himself."

"I'm sure he is," Eleanor had drawled with an obvious lack of enthusiasm.

"Oh, something's wrong, isn't it? Things aren't what they seem, are they, my lady? He may be happy, but you're not. Oh, no, what's his lordship going to do to you now?"

"It appears I'm to be wagered in a game of chance."

"He can't do that. Can he?"

"Sad to say, I believe he can," Eleanor had replied with a sigh. "As a woman I've no independent rights, and as a daughter, obedience is expected of me. My father may do what he wishes with me."

"And you're going to give up just like that?"

In spite of it all, Eleanor had smiled. "From that question can I assume that you hope I've some plan to thwart my father?"

Jilly nodded. "Do you, my lady?"

"Yes, and if I hope to succeed then I must appear to go along with him. It shall be a ruse, nothing more, I assure you. I shall comply with my father's orders to dress and go downstairs, but with your help I shall slip through the garden into the alley and before dawn I shall be away from him forever."

"With my help, my lady?" There had been a squeak of hesitancy in this query.

"Yes, Jilly. I need your help. I shall depend on you to make certain the ballroom doors to the garden are open. You will do it, won't you?"

"Yes, my lady. But where will you go?"

"To the Duchess of Exeter. And you mustn't worry, Jilly, for I shan't leave you behind. Once you've opened the doors, wait for me by the alley gate."

With Jilly's promise to open the ballroom doors, Eleanor's belief that she would free herself this night gave her ample fortitude to descend the wide sweep of stairs beside her father and sit in the vestibule like a thoroughbred on display at Tattersall's.

All around her the swarm of gamesters and sightseers discoursed as if she were invisible. She'd never heard such demeaning utterances, never imagined such vulgarities, and although she wished to lash at them in a fiery tirade, her gaze remained averted as she feigned disinterest in what was going on.

No matter what they said or did, Eleanor told herself she would not look up until she had achieved unshakable control over her emotions. She couldn't do anything to jeopardize her plan, nor could she let anyone know the true direction of her thoughts. This gathering of rogues and lechers wasn't worthy of her, and she would not give one inch of herself in any way. Even to reveal her revulsion of them would be too generous. Anger and disdain and, yes, fear seethed through Eleanor, but these men would never see any of that, she vowed with silent determination as she focused on her hands resting upon her lap. They trembled a bit, and she paid undue attention to smoothing out the skirt of her gown as she bit her lower lip to prevent herself from saying something she might regret.

Her father finished summarizing the rules. The

last player took his seat at the table, and Eleanor
willed herself to show no emotion. Slowly, the fire
drained from Eleanor's eyes, her jaw relaxed, and
although she was furious, her features dissolved
into a bland unreadable expression. She heard the
players being announced by her father's majordomo. Although everyone already knew one another, this introduction was a requisite formality.
To her father's right sat the Duke of Marlbor-
ough's brother, Lord Robert Spencer; next came
Lord Skeffington; then Captain Whimper; one of
the Rugby lordlings, Westbridge; and finally,
someone with the unlikely name of Lord Fortune
completed the circle, sitting on her father's left.

What manner of man would be so craven to sit
at her father's game table? Eleanor wondered, but
she didn't look up as the cards were dealt, brandy
was poured, and the game began. They were all
aristocrats, except perhaps for Captain Whimper
and Lord Fortune whose names had to be con-
trived. Her thoughts flew back to that evening
when she'd overheard Lady Soames gossiping
about Lord Fortune. How unutterably naive she'd
been to feel sorry for anyone called Lord Fortune.
Obviously, those vicious tattlemongers had known
of what they spoke. They'd said he owned no conscience. What had happened to honor? Or was the
sad truth that all men were as low as her father?
Eleanor closed her eyes and images of Mr. Weare
crossed her mind's canvas. No, all men were not
dishonorable, and Eleanor had only to recall Mr.
Weare to know that it was not foolish to believe.

A cheer echoed through the vestibule. The first
hand was completed. Lord Fortune had won, and
this seemed to please the crowd immensely.
Eleanor suppressed her natural curiosity to peek
at the men and continued to focus upon her
hands.

Captain Whimper won the next three games,

and after only forty minutes, Lord Skeffington was out of the play altogether. At an hour and a half, Westbridge was out. After that Eleanor's father won twice in a row, then he failed to take a trick in the next hand and grumbled a string of oaths Eleanor was glad she couldn't understand. Lord Spencer was the third player to be cleaned out.

From somewhere deep inside the town house a clock chimed twice. There were three hours remaining to sunrise, and there were three players still in the game. Ten minutes later Mulgrave was out of the play.

It was Captain Whimper against Lord Fortune.

At this point, not a soul had a jot of interest in Lady Eleanor. Silence descended on the vestibule, and for the first time since taking her seat, Eleanor dared to tilt her head upwards to peek from beneath lowered lashes. As she suspected, every eye was focused on the gamesters. It was almost as if they'd forgotten she was there. It was now or never, if she intended to make an escape. She was going to slip out for a breath of air on the ballroom balcony—that's what she would tell her father, if he asked where she was going.

She rose from her seat and pivoted toward the corridor that led into the ballroom. She would have to walk behind the gaming table, and as her gaze moved past the table's remaining occupants, her heart leapt and then plummeted in a violent contraction. A short gasp of recognition followed this sensation of actual pain as she stared at Mr. Weare sitting opposite a heavyset creature in canary yellow.

Eleanor's hands flew upward and she pressed her fingers to her mouth. For several moments, she seemed to cease breathing, and when she finally exhaled and took her next breath she collapsed back into the chair, her gaze glued to Mr. Weare, her heart aching in confusion and betrayal.

He was dressed in evening wear, his black jacket unbuttoned to reveal a gold and cream brocade waistcoat. Although his garb was formal, his elaborate neckcloth had been loosened, giving a relaxed, almost insolent impression to his appearance. He looked like a man who cared little for others' opinions, a rebel who existed outside the bounds of decency. His elegant clothes spoke of wealth, and the topaz buttons of his waistcoat sparkled at Eleanor in mockery. No simple gentleman—such as she had believed Mr. Weare to be—could afford such finery, and another pang of confusion beset her.

Although those clear blue eyes, that thick blonde hair and those lean sculptured features were Mr. Weare's, there was much about this man that transformed him into someone else before her eyes. It wasn't fair. He looked like the man who had pledged to be her friend, a man she'd believed knew the meaning of the word honor, the man she'd thought worthy of her trust. But Eleanor knew he wasn't that. Quite to the contrary, there could be nothing trustworthy or honorable about any man who was here in her father's vestibule, at ease and comfortable with this unsavory gathering. The man seated before her could be naught but a knave of the lowest order.

Which one was he? she wondered as misery tore at her heart. Was he Captain Whimper? Or did the erstwhile, traitorous Mr. Weare call himself Lord Fortune? There was a constriction in her throat, for the unfortunate truth was that it really didn't make any difference. Either way Mr. Weare wasn't the man he had pretended to be. He was a rogue as vile as her father. He was one of her father's cronies, a villain so black-hearted that he would sit at the gaming table this night and wager for human flesh. And to think it was those afternoons with Mr. Weare that had kept her from fleeing her father's household when she should have. It was her evolving relationship with Mr. Weare that had lulled her into a false sense of complacency. And then there was that stupid girlish fantasy about one of King Richard's knights. Somehow, somewhere in her mind Mr. Weare and that knight had become too close, and as a result she'd been blinded into attributing to Mr. Weare finer qualities than he merited.

At that instant, Eleanor knew only one desire. She wished to strike out and hurt him as he'd hurt her. If he was closer, she would have slapped him across both cheeks and vented her fury with a catalog of unladylike accusations. None of that was possible. Instead her lips trembled, her eyes and nose burned from the threatened onset of tears, and she pressed her fingers against her mouth to stop the trembling and fight back the tears.

I will not cry. I will not cry. Eleanor repeated this silent litany as her well-developed skills at hiding any trace of emotion took over, but it was too late.

Litchfield had heard her little gasp, and, glancing up from the cards fanned out in his hand, he saw the flash of horror in her gaze as it rested upon him.

Not now, he wanted to call out to her. His eyes took in the agony of her expression. *Don't look at me now. Not like that. Not with such pain and loathing.*

It had been a relief to Litchfield that she'd kept her gaze averted from the gaming table. Thus far his concentration had not wavered from the play, and now, when it was more crucial than ever not to lose a trick, he didn't wish to have his attention diverted. Although he tried to look away, he couldn't tear his gaze from hers. He'd seen the flash of recognition cross her face, followed by a stricken expression. Those exotic eyes widened, then narrowed as her mouth snapped shut and her jaw stiffened. Yet now there was nothing there. Her features were aloof and controlled. He knew she was angry, and no doubt she must be frightened and humiliated, but there wasn't any suggestion of emotion upon her sweet face.

Their past came back to him in a flood of memories, especially that afternoon when she had hinted at some unfortunate secret, something from which she wished to escape, from which to be rescued. The urge to offer the comfort of his arms was fierce. He understood now why she had not hopped around a Christmas tree, had not been spoiled, or told by a doting papa how lovely she was. All that was going to change. He would rescue her. That's why he'd taken a seat at the table, and he would succeed. He longed to hold her to him and whisper in her ear that she had nothing to fear, he longed to feel her relax against him as she had during the wagon ride back to town. He'd sensed her trust that night. It had been a wonderful thing, and now he wanted to hold her again, to experience that trust once more.

But the timing wasn't right. The game was still in progress. More importantly, he hadn't succeeded yet, that trust wasn't yet his to claim, and Litchfield had to force himself to turn back to his cards.

This could be it—the last hand. There were three tricks remaining, but Litchfield had only enough cash to afford two loos while Captain Whimper still had three hundred pounds on the leather-topped table. If Litchfield took the tricks, Captain Whimper would be cleaned out, and it would be over. On the other hand, if he made even the slightest mistake, Captain Whimper would win. Litchfield couldn't concentrate on anything other than the game. He couldn't lose. He could not allow Captain Whimper to get his hands on Lady Eleanor.

Captain Whimper took the first trick, Litchfield the second. They were dead even, and there was an explosive break in the silence. Pandemonium spread through the vestibule as the onlookers placed wagers on the final outcome of the game. It took several minutes for the clamor to die down, and then there was silence again as the crowd pressed closer to the table.

On the count of three, the two men revealed their last cards. Cheers echoed through the vestibule. Lord Fortune had won.

Litchfield smiled. Satisfaction and relief were evident upon his features as he looked toward her, but instead of the gratitude he had expected to see there was only fury upon her countenance. What was wrong with her? Didn't she understand what had happened? Didn't she comprehend how close she had come to being consigned to the proverbial fate worse than death? Had she no notion how foul and degenerate a creature Captain Whimper was?

"Congratulations, Fortune!" Boulton gave Litchfield a hearty slap on the back. "You always did have the devil's own luck."

He didn't reply as he studied Mulgrave's daughter, searching for some sign of appreciation. Bloody damn, but it wasn't there. Not even the slightest inclination of her head, nor a lowering of her lashes as a silent method of communication. Perhaps she was too overwhelmed by everything that had happened.

"What I wouldn't give for a chance at a wench like that," one of the Rugby lordlings said.

Litchfield didn't take his eyes off her. He acknowledged these remarks with a curt nod and stood, his gaze never wavering from hers. The crowd parted to make a path toward Lady Eleanor, and he strode around the table straight to her.

"When you're through with the chit, I'd be happy to take her off your hands," said Captain Whimper. "I've a particular fondness for skin like Devon cream, and I'm wondering if those pretty shoulders are as soft as they look."

Litchfield was near enough to Eleanor to witness how this tasteless remark affected her. Although the facade did not slip from her face, dots of bright pink appeared on her cheeks. He saw her facial muscles tense, her eyelashes flutter closed, and he felt her mortification as she raised her arms to cross them over the expanse of fair skin revealed by the decolleté bodice. If only he could ease her humiliation. If only he could make everything right for her, he wished, giving not a moment's pause to this uncharacteristic thought.

"What do you intend with her?"

Litchfield didn't reply. He stopped before the lady and executed a perfectly proper leg.

"Good evening, Lady Eleanor. I am at your service, my lady," said Litchfield. Their eyes met, their gazes locked. Although she might succeed in hiding her feelings from the others, he knew the true direction of her thoughts when he watched those familiar golden dots rise in her eyes, and he couldn't stop himself from grinning. She was as furious with him as she was with her father and the rest of this motley crew, and for some insane reason this pleased him. After all, he mused, it was far better than seeing no reaction from her whatsoever.

"Tell us, Fortune," Boulton urged. "What will you do with your prize?"

"Yes, tell us. You mustn't keep us in suspense another moment."

That was a damn good question. He'd rescued her from Whimper, but what would he do with her now? An even better question was: did the lady even care what he did? Truth to tell, she probably wished never to set eyes on him after this night. Litchfield wasn't a fool. He had a pretty good idea that he'd disillusioned her already, and he cursed himself. It was obvious she considered him no better than the likes of Mulgrave and Whimper. *But it isn't true*, he wanted to call out to her. He wanted to convince her that he was better than either of them. Or at least he could be, for she'd brought that out in him. Each day, each hour, each minute spent with her had resurrected within him a goodness and gentleness, an honor he had long thought dead. After all, he hadn't seduced her as he'd first intended. Furthermore, he'd come to appreciate her for something more than an enticing pair of breasts and moist red lips. Why, he'd only entered the game tonight to rescue her, not to possess her or demean her. And if she didn't appreciate all that he'd done for her, then he'd have to do something else to prove himself to her.

His mind raced over the possibilities, the foremost being that he must remove her from her father's household. What future could there be for her after tonight? No gentleman would have her once news of this evening spread through Mayfair. By noon every lady in the West End would be whispering behind her fan about Lady Eleanor. The servants would talk, she would be turned away from Almack's and every respectable drawing room, and she would be cut direct, indirect, and sublime should she dare to show her face.

There was no future for Mulgrave's daughter save with him. He could make everything right for her, and that wasn't just a wish. It was within his power. He could protect her from Whimper and her father. He could protect her from the scandalmongers. He thought of the little he knew about her, the gossip he'd heard from Boulton and what he'd gleaned from their conversations, and he knew he could offer her something better than the past nineteen years. He could rescue her from an existence that promised naught but shame and loneliness. He could give her a future.

"Indeed, Fortune, what are your plans for my daughter?"

And no one waited with more expectation for his reply than did Eleanor. She shouldn't care, she told herself. She should leave now, an inner voice prompted. Jilly was waiting by the garden gate. But she didn't leave. Instead she, too, waited for his reply.

Eleven

"I INTEND TO marry the lady," Litchfield stated without a breath of hesitation.

Astonishment reverberated through the vestibule.

"Bloody hell, you say," Captain Whimper swore in disappointment.

"Marry Eleanor?" Mulgrave couldn't believe what he'd heard. "You don't have to do *that*."

"What did you expect?"

"But legshackled? It's been a long night. You can reconsider in the light of day. None of us will hold you to such a hasty declaration."

Litchfield, however, didn't hear any of this. His attention was focused on nothing but Mulgrave's daughter as he studied her face, searching for her reaction. Again he expected to see relief. At the least, gratitude. But neither of those appeared. For the second time in as many minutes, her mouth dropped open in a clear indication of astonishment, and frustration tugged at Litchfield's heart as she turned from him to flee from the vestibule with a sound that might have been a sob. She had made it abundantly clear that she wanted nothing to do with him.

"Spirited thing," chuckled Whimper.

"Quite the hoyden, Fortune," drawled Lambe. "Appears you've got your work cut out for you."

"Cut line," Litchfield snapped, his frustration with her reaction escalating. This was a disaster. It was getting worse by the second. He had to follow her. He had to change her mind and make her understand why he'd done this.

Mulgrave swore. "Damn the chit. Don't know what's gotten into her. I'll get her, Fortune. Don't you worry. She knows how to be obedient."

"That's all right, Mulgrave. Your help isn't needed. I'll go after her myself." Litchfield paused beneath the arched doorway that led out of the rotunda to look over his shoulder. His jaw tightened, and he went white with anger as he lanced the earl with his sharp blue eyes. For a moment it looked as if he might cross the vestibule to shake Mulgrave by the lapels. There was such fury etched upon Litchfield's features that the Marquis of Lambe, who was standing nearest to him, actually backed away to safety. "By the bye, Mulgrave, I don't want you within ten leagues of her. Never again," Litchfield concluded between clenched teeth.

He didn't bother to wait for an acknowledgment and in several quick strides had made his way to a ballroom at the end of the corridor where the faint light of a new dawn peeped between the heavy draperies. At the far end of the room a pair of French doors had been flung wide, where he spotted her standing on a balcony staring up at the sky. As he crossed to the open doors, his footsteps echoed through the cavernous room, and when he reached the threshold she spun around to glare at him.

"You!" she exclaimed. It was an accusation. Her hands were planted akimbo, and she looked like some ancient goddess of fury.

For an instant Litchfield was caught off guard,

then his eyes began to twinkle. "Yes, it's me." He couldn't help grinning at the hostility that made her eyes sparkle like gold dust, and when she opened her mouth as if to speak, he held up a hand to stop her. "You needn't say a word, for I know exactly what you'll say."

"Do you know?" she challenged with a toss of her head.

"I'm a depraved rogue, and what I did was worse than seduction. I deceived you, and you loath me, hate me, want nothing to do with me. I even suspect that you're going to try to tell me you had some scheme of your own to save yourself this night. And, no doubt, in addition to all my other sins I'm guilty of having spoiled your plans."

Her black brows arched upward like ravens taking flight. What he said reminded her of those times when they—Mr. Weare and Miss Carew—had seemed to know what the other was thinking. She'd liked it then, but they weren't those people any longer, and it infuriated her to think that he might know what she was planning.

"How dare you mock me!" she hissed at him.

"Mock you? Never. I have naught but respect for you. You should have seen yourself in there. You were splendid, you know. Positively magnificent." His voice fell to a whisper as he stepped onto the balcony, toward her. She was trembling, perhaps from the early morning chill, perhaps from her anger, and he thought she was more beautiful than ever. He drank in the sight of that Gypsy black hair tumbling about creamy shoulders. One glossy strand taunted him as it twisted and curled to fall into the gentle dip between her breasts. He still wanted her more than any other woman he'd known, and he knew with sudden clarity how right he'd been not to seduce and then discard this woman as if she had no value. Miss

Nora Carew or Lady Eleanor or whatever she wished to call herself had infinite value as a woman of beauty and courage and passion. She was a prize worthy of any man. He moved closer. She backed away. He took another step forward, and she continued to move backwards until she was pressed up against the marble balustrade. She couldn't go any farther, and he gave her a gentle smile.

"What were you thinking about out here?" he asked softly. "Besides all that anger for me?"

That deep velvety voice worked its magic on Eleanor, and her anger started to fade. "I was looking at the stars in the sky," she whispered in shy reply and dropped her gaze from his. Her heart was hammering. She wasn't supposed to feel like this around him. He wasn't supposed to affect her this way. She should hate him and his nearness should make her skin crawl with loathing, but that didn't happen. Instead his voice made her limbs go weak, and all she could think of was how he had made her feel before. Too well did she remember how pleasurable it had been to catch him stealing a glance at her. Too well did she recall how his lingering touch had left her wanting more.

"Stars? That's a relief." His voice was husky. "And I thought you were thinking of all the different ways you could skewer me alive."

Eleanor didn't want to look at him and smile, but she did. She didn't want to confide in him, but she did, and it terrified her because she didn't know why.

"There are so many of them up there," she heard herself say. "Stars, that is. They go on and on into infinity. It made me think about all the things I'll never have. All the possibilities that I've lost."

Something tightened in his chest. He didn't like

to hear that melancholy little catch in her voice, and again he wanted nothing more than to take her in his arms and comfort her until everything was right. But he suspected she'd fight him off. Instead he dared to reach out and cup her chin to better gaze into her eyes.

"You make the future sound a forbidding and lonely thing. But it doesn't have to be like that. There are stars in your eyes, you know. It's those little golden flecks, they're the stars, and when I look at them I don't think of all the possibilities I've lost. I see all the possibilities I've found. I think the future could be endless and bright with a thousand possibilities we've yet to imagine."

Her chin trembled as he stroked it with the pad of his thumb. The gentleness of his words matched his tender caress. A warning bell went off inside her, and she tried to move away, but there wasn't any place for her to go. She was pressed against the balustrade. "That sounds like seduction." Her voice was shaky and unsure.

"A gentleman can't seduce his betrothed," he said as if nothing else mattered and life were truly that simple.

She was taken aback. "You're not really going to marry me, are you?" The man was a scoundrel, no better than her father, who'd been ill-suited to being a husband.

"Gather up what you'll need for the night. I'll send someone for the rest of your things in the morning."

"You didn't answer my question, sir." She tried to sound bolder than she really felt. "Are you going to marry me?"

He ran a hand across his eyes, wishing that he knew what to say. Of course, he wanted to rescue her from Mulgrave. Of course, he wanted her to have the happiness that had eluded her. And when he'd said he would marry her, he'd meant it.

But the truth was he'd never intended to marry anyone. He wasn't that sort of man. He wouldn't be a good husband, and she deserved the best. Verily, the proposition rather terrified him, but he wasn't going to tell her. Not yet, at least. Once again, he didn't answer her. "You're coming with me," was the best he could reply.

"Why?" she demanded, her anger resurfacing. She clenched her fists and taunted, "Because you own me?"

"No."

"Why then? Give me a good reason."

"Because I would never let any woman spend another night in this household," he said the one thing that rang true.

"And your household is any better?"

This barb hit its mark, and he gave a tired sigh. He didn't want to fight with her.

"Think of me what you will. Most of it is probably true, and as time passes you'll likely hear much more to displease you about my past. But never forget—no matter what you hear—I would never demean a woman, no less my own daughter, as your father did this night, and having said so is my pledge, for no matter what, I am a man of my word. You are in my care now, and I will guard your honor at all cost." His velvety voice rang with a conviction that was unsettling.

Eleanor trembled. She wanted to trust him. She wanted to surrender to his care. But how could she? There wasn't any Mr. Weare. The man she thought she'd come to know and trust was really the Earl of Litchfield. *Lord Fortune.* She was deathly afraid of being hurt, afraid of expecting too much, of hoping for happiness and like her mother being left with nothing. "God help me, but I want to believe you," she whispered in a voice so quiet he had to strain to hear it.

"But you don't?"

"Of course not. How could you expect otherwise?" How could he look so innocent, as if there were no reason for her not to believe him? Was he so depraved that he didn't comprehend the magnitude of his transgression? Just looking at him was making her angry, for it seemed as if he was waiting for her approval. Her fury boiled over. "May you rot in eternal damnation for what you've done to me!"

"What was that?"

"You made me trust you! How can you ever expect me to trust you again after the way you lied to me, *Lord Fortune?*"

He winced as if she'd struck him a physical blow. "It's only a nickname. I am Addison Weare, the Earl of Litchfield. I didn't lie to you."

"Hah! You don't call what you did lying?"

"I prefer to think of it as omitting a fact. And while we're tossing accusations about, need I remind you that I wasn't the only one to lie, *Miss Carew.*" In his next breath, he regretted having said this, for he had a very good idea why she wouldn't have wanted to tell him her real name. So much had been explained with the simple knowledge that Mulgrave was her parent. To realize the weight of her burden hit him hard. Young ladies in their first Season were meant to enjoy the social whirl without being the victim of gossip. Young ladies were meant to be surrounded by eager suitors, but from what Litchfield recalled of Polite Society he suspected she had probably been snubbed on more than one occasion. Her deception had been innocent, and he guessed that she had wanted nothing more than to be herself without the stigma of her father hovering over her. She didn't deserve his accusations, and he said, "I'm sorry. That was uncalled for."

Eleanor's heart somersaulted. Why was he being so kind? So sympathetic? She hadn't expected an apology. She'd expected hostility, and a spate of questions that didn't come. Maybe she wanted that, for she could better deal with honest anger than with patience. Why wasn't he berating her? She stared at him, unaware of how telling was the confusion upon her face.

"I'm sure you had your reasons," he said. "Perhaps someday you'll trust me enough to tell me why. In the meantime, you're still coming with me. And don't be stubborn about it. It's late, and we're both too tired to make any other decisions. There will be plenty of time tomorrow to talk this through."

She nodded her assent. He was right, of course. She couldn't stay here, and although she didn't even know what she should call him, for now leaving with him was the best choice.

He took off his jacket to drape it over her shoulders. Although she was exquisite in that gold satin gown, it was a reminder of how Boulton and Whimper and the rest had stared at her with lust in their eyes. It wasn't proper, and he buttoned the jacket close across the revealing neckline.

Again, there was a fluttering in Eleanor's heart. Touched by his gesture, she looked up at him and something inside her melted. How right he was. She was so exhausted that she actually wished she could collapse against his chest and cry her eyes out. She required several moments to compose herself. "Could we stay just a few minutes more?"

"Whatever for?"

"I've never seen the sun rise."

It was a simple little thing, yet it affected him profoundly. "Of course," he replied, knowing there was much she'd never had and which she deserved to experience.

They stood side by side on the balcony. The slender young woman in gold with black hair and the tall golden-haired man wearing black. From the street below, the voices of the gentlemen departing the town house mingled with the early morning sounds of the metropolis. There was the heavy clip-clop of draught horses pulling an ice wagon, a cock's crow from a nearby carriage house, the whistle of the lamplighter extinguishing lanterns, and above it all the gray sky was turning to silver.

He wished he could put his arm around her, but he feared she might pull away, so he stood as close to her as he could, and after a sideways glance to reassure himself she was at ease he raised his face to the eastern skyline. The sun cracked over the rooftops to bathe them in its warmth and light, and Litchfield sighed, experiencing a transformation within himself. Something was different. He was feeling again, and to his surprise, he quite liked it.

Twelve

THE FIRST THING Litchfield thought of when he woke up shortly before noon the next day was his mother seated before her easel in the rose garden at Litchfield Park. He saw her as if it were yesterday, and he heard her as clearly as if she were alive and well and there in his London bedchamber at that precise moment.

You must promise me, darling boy, to find happiness . . . and you must remember that where there is love one is never alone.

At last he understood what his mother had meant. He understood why it was he had been living such a reckless life, and for the first time in many years, the long-denied unbearable weight of loneliness pressed upon his heart.

He'd lost his faith that autumn night sixteen years before in the rose garden, and without hope he'd submerged himself in a vicious cycle that had denied anything beyond the moment at hand. He hadn't allowed himself to feel, and in doing so he'd turned away from the goodness one derived from being connected with another soul. He had not believed in love. Love didn't last. He believed in nothing beyond the present. He'd denied his feelings, his needs, and the future, and he had de-

137

nied how truly lonely he'd become. Until Mulgrave's daughter.

Sitting up and swinging his feet over the side of his bed, Litchfield pushed several strands of blonde hair off his brow as the vision of his mother faded away and in its place rose a vision of the young lady he'd brought home with him at dawn. Somehow Mulgrave's daughter had broken through the barriers. He was feeling again. Although he'd only come to realize that fact at sunrise this day, it had happened some time ago, creeping up on him as mysteriously as the sun crept over the rooftops of Mayfair. Mulgrave's daughter had come knocking upon his heart. She'd unlocked the past, and in doing so had caused his defenses to melt away. There was no denying he'd come to value and cherish her. He knew the truth. She was his future. He needed her, and he must do everything within his power to win her, for without Mulgrave's daughter his heart would freeze over once again and he would be destined to naught but loneliness.

Litchfield mulled over the events of last evening. One thing was clear. No such tender emotions had come knocking upon her heart as they had upon his. She had made it clear the low regard in which she held him, and it was hard to credit that he'd actually gotten her to leave her father's town house in his company. Litchfield's only shred of hope was that there had been something special growing between them when they'd been nothing more than Mr. Weare and Miss Carew, something real that must surely have sustained a tiny space in her heart. Something waiting to be found and given life. Litchfield could only hope that with the proper measure of nurturing those fragile bonds might resurface and flourish. The task of winning Mulgrave's daughter would be a daunting one, but he would start with the little everyday things, and, with the intention of spoiling and cosseting her, he flew into a frenzy of activity.

"The flowers?" Litchfield inquired of his valet. He had been giving orders for three-quarters of an hour, and as his valet helped him into his waist-coat Litchfield wanted to make certain those orders were being followed. "Were you able to get fresh flowers?"

"Yes, my lord. They're already in the Chinese guest room. Yellow roses and lilies, precisely as you requested. Four large arrangements."

"And the soaps? The linens? They're the finest in the house? In London?"

"Of course, my lord. What was not on the premises has been obtained from the most exclusive purveyors."

"And Lady Eleanor's breakfast. Did she order a tray?"

"Not yet, my lord. I'm informed that Lady Eleanor is still asleep, but her abigail indicates it is her mistress's custom to take two toasted cinnamon buns, a small serving of fruit, and a cup of chocolate upon rising."

Litchfield experienced a momentary twinge of panic. He couldn't recall the last time he'd imbibed anything as tame as chocolate. "Chocolate? Was there any in the pantry?"

"No, sir, but not to worry. A footman was dispatched posthaste to the Exchange, and there are now several tins on the pantry shelves."

"Imported Belgain, I trust."

"Of course, sir, and powdered Swiss and bitter-sweet Italian. I've informed the staff of your wishes. *Only the finest* for Lady Eleanor. And your instructions are being executed to the letter. The modiste on Upper Mount Street has already delivered a selection of gowns and accessories which I'm assured are as proper as they are stylish. Cook has consulted with Lady Eleanor's abigail and compiled a list of the lady's favorite dishes. This evening's menu has been prepared accordingly. Roast duckling with a marmalade sauce, a cheese soufflé, poached salmon and steamed vegetables. As for the final item on your list, Mr. Hildebrande at Lock's has sent a response to your missive. A box will be delivered from St. James's, he assures, no later than four o'clock this afternoon. And yes, there will be flowers on Lady Eleanor's breakfast tray."

Litchfield raised his arms as his valet slipped on his jacket. He stared in the mirror while the manservant squared the shoulders and smoothed out the sleeves, and he frowned at his reflection, wondering how it was that he had so much energy after such a long night. And this was only the beginning. He was going to do everything within his power to give Mulgrave's daughter all that she'd been denied, and in doing so, he hoped to become the most important person in her life. She would not be able to consider a future without him any more than he could without her. Litchfield cast a sideways glance at the valet. "You've known me for twenty years, Peters. Do you think I've lost my mind?"

"No, sir." The loyal manservant refrained from stating that the entire household staff was agog with chatter to the contrary. Litchfield's scullery maid had heard from Lady Althorpe's scullery maid who'd heard from the Marquis of Lambe's stable boy about the goings-on at Mulgrave's. The sensational tale had been repeated *ad nauseam*, embellished most dramatically with each retelling, and Litchfield's staff knew the entire story of how their master had rescued the young lady from the clutches of the loathsome Captain Whimper. That particular turn of events would not have been remarkable were it not for that fact that Litchfield had brought Lady Eleanor Villiers to his town house on Langham Place, the house in which his parents had lived as newlyweds and to which Litchfield had never before brought a young woman of any rank or class with the exception of one or two impoverished relations in their dotage. Indeed, the staff, including Peters, considered his lordship's behavior regarding Lady Eleanor most out of the ordinary, and hence, his state of mind unquestionably strange.

"And how went your interview with the abigail, Peters?" Litchfield had instructed Peters to speak with the girl who had accompanied Mulgrave's daughter upon their departure from Curzon Street. "What did she tell you?"

"As you suspicioned, Lady Eleanor is acquainted with the Dowager Duchess of Exeter, my lord. Apparently, Lady Eleanor has been under her grace's wing this Season. Although it was not an official arrangement, I'm assured the dowager duchess looks upon Lady Eleanor as she might her own child."

Litchfield nodded. That was what he'd hoped to learn. It was a relief to know there was someone who cared about Lady Eleanor's welfare and to whom he could turn for advice. Having attended to her immediate comfort, his next order of business was to call upon the Dowager Duchess of Exeter. Hopefully, the venerable lady would assist him in his plans for Mulgrave's daughter.

Confusion was the first thing Eleanor experienced when she awoke later that afternoon upon a strange bed in a strange room, but that quickly changed to an undeniable surge of delight as she surveyed her surroundings. The bedchamber and its furnishings in the popular Chinese tradition, were the most elegant she had ever seen. The bed boasted carved posts featuring a design of entwined ibis, and it was tented with bright gold and plum striped chintz. The damask sheets upon which she had slept smelled of lemon and honeysuckle, as did the bank of lace pillows beneath her head. Other pleasant scents wafted through the colorful room, and, sitting up a bit straighter, she noticed several arrangements of yellow roses and cream-colored lilies which matched the dainty floral motif of the hand-painted wallpaper.

Her gaze took in all the small details that contradicted this was a guest chamber and made her think, instead, this was a room upon which someone had put their own special mark. Before one tall window a pair of doves cooed in a bamboo cage; there were more flowers on a low table set before a floral-patterned settee; several gowns in shades of blue and green were hung on the door of a large armoire; a pretty chip bonnet trimmed with streamers sat upon a rosewood vanity; and upon the beside table was a stack of boots. The spines were turned toward Eleanor, and she read the titles. *A Lady's Travel Diary, Touring in Homer's Footsteps, The Life and Times of a Gentleman Turned Sailor,* and *Exploring the Mysteries of Palestine.*

After the nightmare of last evening, this was like a dream, an extraordinarily wonderful dream from which she never wished to awaken. All the negative emotions faded away in this setting. Animosity, defeat, and betrayal could not sustain themselves when Eleanor glanced about the gold and plum room and asked herself whose dresses those were, whose bonnet. Where did the books come from? Why the doves? Why the abundance of flowers? There was only one explanation, only one way that intriguing stack of books or that chip bonnet had come to be there.

It was him. Litchfield. Weare. Fortune. He'd done this for her, and the realization pushed her suddenly close to foolish tears.

There were so many unanswered questions, or, more specifically, answers of which Eleanor was afraid. Why hadn't she fled into the garden last night? Some force over which she had no control had made her pause to look at the stars, as if she were waiting for him. It shouldn't have been like that. Something had happened to the single-minded resolve that had sustained her for so many years. She shouldn't have waited, nor should she own anything but unfavorable thoughts of Litchfield. But that wasn't the case, and she wasn't sure she wanted to understand why it was that the pleasant memories burned more brightly upon her memory than did his abuse of her trust. Nor why, pray tell, she was so touched by this pretty room. It was that. Just a pretty show of fabric and flowers, a few books. Nothing more. Still it caused her eyes to mist with hot tears, and it prevented her from dressing with all haste to flee this house before she might encounter *him* again.

The door opened and her heart leapt, then settled. It was only Jilly.

"Good afternoon, my lady," Jilly bubbled. "You're awake at last. And how are you feeling this afternoon?"

"Somewhat as if I'm caught in a dream," Eleanor confessed, sitting up to receive the breakfast tray across her lap.

"It is lovely here, isn't it?" Jilly took the lid off a plate of cinnamon buns and poured Eleanor a cup of chocolate. "His lordship's staff has been busy since we arrived. Tippy-toeing in and out even while you were sleeping, my lady. First it was the flowers, then the doves and the books, and finally, the clothes. They even changed the cushions in the window seats and on the settee. Twice they changed them until someone said the brocade ones were prettiest."

"What a lot of bother," Eleanor essayed an indif-

ferent tone. It shouldn't make any difference how
much attention was being paid to her. The man
had betrayed her. He was a cad, a scoundrel, and
it was obvious he was endeavoring to bribe his
way into her good graces. She took a sip of the
frothy hot chocolate and recognized the superior
blend. It was Berengere's, so expensive that she
and Lady Penelope had enjoyed it only on special
occasions. Yes, he was most assuredly trying to
bribe her.

"Oh, no. No bother at all. Mrs. Harmon, the
housekeeper, said nothing was too good for the future mistress. I'm so happy for you, my lady.
You're to be married!"

"We shall see."

This cryptic remark confused Jilly, and she
paused in the task of tying back the draperies.
"But, my lady, Mrs. Harmon was telling me that
his lordship dictated an announcement for *The
Times*, and he's going to consult with Mr. Gunther
in Berkeley Square about wedding confections.
Lord Litchfield is seeming a might certain for you
to be sounding otherwise. He's telling the world,
you know, and Mrs. Harmon says the first of the
banns will be ready this Sunday."

"And he also told me his name was Mr. Weare,"
came Eleanor's sharp retort. "Lord Litchfield was
the gentleman I was visiting in Bloomsbury, although he never hinted that he possessed a title,
or wealth, or a reputation of any note. Lord
Litchfield is not at all the gentleman I thought he
was, and I see no reason to trust him or think that
anything he says regarding my future can be relied upon."

"Well, at least you've left your father's house,
my lady, and Lord Litchfield does seem a nice
man."

"People aren't always what they seem."

"And what's wrong with that, my lady? Take

me, for example. If a stranger saw me walking through the park, they'd think I was nothing more than an uneducated serving girl from Limehouse, but, truth is, I can read and do my numbers. You haven't forgotten how you've been telling me not to judge a book by its cover, have you?" Jilly offered this fervent challenge to her mistress.

"Are you suggesting that I give Lord Litchfield a chance to prove himself?"

"Something like that."

"Well, go on, Jilly, explain yourself," Eleanor prompted. Although she'd never imagined being in a position to receive counsel from her abigail, she was of a fair mind and willing to listen. "I've a feeling there's something more you'd like to tell me."

"Well, my lady, it's just that when you were in your father's house it was a good idea to think about leaving. It was like you were always saying. You were living at the whim of an unkind and unpredictable man. Then anything was better, but in this household it's different. A body can tell a lot just by listening to what's being said below stairs, and here, everyone likes Lord Litchfield. No one's afraid of being thrown in the street or getting a beating. I've got a clean sunny room on the other side of your dressing room, and well, you see—" Here, Jilly hesitated in her speech to shift from one foot to the other in a show of nervousness. "Well, I know I've got you to thank for bringing me with you when you left your father's and I ought to be loyal no matter what, but, truth is, I'm not leaving here."

Eleanor remained silent, and the young woman continued.

"Think about it, my lady. What do you know of the real world?" Jilly's words were harsh, but there was no disrespect intended, and their passion captured Eleanor's attention. "You think it's something wonderful, something to do with free choice and independence, but I've lived on my own and I don't know anything about such high-minded things. What I know about isn't pleasant. Tell me, my lady, what experience do you have with the streets or fending for yourself? Have you ever gone to sleep hungry? I know what it's like, and I don't wish to struggle, nor be cold and dirty and hungry with nothing to show for twelve hours' toiling excepting an empty stomach, raw hands and an aching back."

Eleanor didn't know what to say. The truth of what Jilly said was brutal, and Eleanor couldn't help feeling incredibly selfish and simpleminded. No matter what it had been like for Lady Penelope under her father's domination, it was nothing compared to struggling for one's next meal or a safe place to spend the night.

Jilly started to apologize. "Begging your pardon, my lady, I know it isn't my place to speak of—"

"No, don't take back what you said," Eleanor cut her off. "I'm glad you spoke your mind, Jilly."

The abigail curtsied. "Does that mean you'll give his lordship a chance?"

"Yes, and I'll try not to do anything foolish or precipitous. Although I'm not promising there shall be any wedding."

"Oh, my lady, that's a good enough promise for me." Jilly bobbed another curtsy. "You've done so much to change my life, my lady, and I'll be ever so grateful to think I might give a little something in return."

With a final nod, Eleanor managed to conclude this particular conversation. Once again the two young women were mistress and servant as Eleanor finished her chocolate and cinnamon buns and Jilly retrieved one of the gowns from the armoire and set it across the bed along with matching slippers and a light shawl.

"Tell me, Jilly, what is expected of me this afternoon?" asked Eleanor. Having finished her chocolate, she left the tented bed and crossed to the washstand, her bare feet padding on the luxurious carpet.

"Lord Litchfield asked to be informed once you were up and dressed. You're to meet his lordship in the library as soon as possible."

"Then prepare to meet him I shall," Eleanor said, forcing herself not to consider what he might intend, or how she would react upon seeing him in the light of day in his own home. She splashed water on her face, and with Jilly's aid dressed to go downstairs and meet him.

The rest of Lord Litchfield's town house was a shocking contrast to the gold and plum Chinese bedchamber. Devoid of any personal touches, it gave the impression that no one lived there. There were no flowers or tabletop portraits in the corridors as there were at Exeter House or as Lady Penelope had scattered throughout Mulgrave Manor, and the library, in particular, was barren and unwelcoming. Nothing was out of place, not even a bundle of unread correspondence or a book left open upon a chair. It reminded Eleanor of a bank, cold and impersonal, and she couldn't help wondering with sadness if the gentleman who called this home was as cold. It was a tragic thing to consider, and a tiny perplexed frown creased Eleanor's brow when the majordomo announced her arrival.

Litchfield turned toward the door. He had been standing before one of the tall windows, perhaps watching the activity in the street, perhaps staring at nothing, for his expression when he welcomed Eleanor was unreadable. He inquired whether her room was satisfactory.

"Yes, it's lovely," replied Eleanor, finding scant

comfort in the fact that they were behaving like virtual strangers. Too much had passed between them. She, for one, would speak her mind.

Litchfield escorted Eleanor to a chair, then closed the library door and went to stand beside his desk. For several ticks of the mantle clock, he stared at Eleanor. Her loveliness filled his eyes. She was a bright Gypsy beauty in a mauve silk gown, and he was struck by how dull his home must seem to her.

Eleanor spoke first. "Am I your prisoner?" she asked. There was nothing unfriendly about the manner in which she posed this question; it was merely something she wished to know.

Litchfield tried not to reveal how deeply this question touched him. *Prisoner.* The very use of the word made him recoil. It also made him think of all those things he would give her, and all those ways in which Mulgrave had failed her but he could make right. *Prisoner.* Verily, he wished she had not been so forthright, for he did not intend to be entirely honest with her. He knew why she had no dreams save those of independence, and he was ashamed of his reaction to her question. He couldn't help himself, but his first thought was that he wished she *were* his prisoner. He was afraid of losing her, but he knew that to hold her by force would smother any possibility he might have of keeping her.

"No, you're not a prisoner. You're free to leave any time you like, for the afternoon or for good," he said, because he knew how important it was to distance himself from Mulgrave and all that her father represented in her mind. He knew how she valued her freedom. He would not deny her that, and, having made such a difficult declaration, he waited for her reply. ·

"Thank you," Eleanor whispered. It was more of a sigh than an actual statement. Her tone was soft, and her expression reflected genuine relief. She took a fortifying breath and forced herself to voice another truth she couldn't deny. "And thank you for last night. I know that I didn't behave as if I were in the least bit grateful, but I do recognize the service you performed in my behalf."

"Yes, well, it's always amazing how a good sleep can put things in perspective." This interview was beginning far better than he'd imagined, and he dared to retrieve something from behind the desk.

"What's this?" Eleanor asked as he handed her a large bandbox. *Lock's* was embossed in gold lettering on the top.

"A betrothal gift," he said in as offhand a manner as he could manage.

She was taken aback. "You're truly determined to marry me?"

"I take it the notion doesn't thrill you?"

"I hadn't planned on marrying anyone." She couldn't prevent a childlike note of truculence from coloring this reply.

"Ah, yes. You were intent upon a life of adventures and independence. Well, you know, I hadn't planned on marrying either, but sometimes things change," he said with infinite patience. "Things over which we have no control. Fate, you know, and I don't believe one can fight Fate."

"My mother believed in Fate," Eleanor heard herself confide, and she couldn't help being incensed with herself and with him and even with her mother. *There's no such thing as a coincidence.* How odd it was to recall that she'd remembered that very quote the first afternoon she'd encountered him at Montague House. If that was true, then all of this had been decreed from the moment they collided. It meant she didn't have any choice in the matter, and considering that possibility, Eleanor's hostility flared.

"Even if Fate is at work, that doesn't change the fact that I don't even like you," Eleanor said. But it wasn't true. She knew that. Despite it all, despite common sense, there were any number of things she liked about him. Still, her indignation didn't stop Eleanor from trying to deflate Litchfield's spirits. Why did he have to be so amiable when she felt so trapped? He appeared unflappable. There wasn't any trace of resentment in what he'd said, and a little devil in Eleanor couldn't help wishing that something might ruin his day. Surely he'd had too much to drink last night, didn't he at least have a tiny headache?

"Well, mayhap you don't like me, but you don't hate me. Or at least I don't think you do."

"You betrayed me," she rejoined, wishing that he wasn't calm and didn't sound so certain of himself. If he hadn't intended on getting wed, he should be angry like she was, not handing out betrothal gifts as if he'd planned on this.

In the face of her accusation, he sustained that composed voice and even managed a smile. "No, I didn't betray you. Not really. You were only betrayed because you thought you know who I was, but the truth is you don't know me at all. Won't you at least give me a chance and get to know me? You liked Mr. Weare, didn't you, and he's part of me. Who knows, you might actually like the rest of me. Even my less than sterling habits. I've been told I can be a wholly charming rascal."

Eleanor couldn't stop herself smiling at this. She wished she could, but it wasn't possible. She didn't want to react this way, but he was right. He *was* a charming rascal, and that was one of the very things she'd liked about him. The way he put her at ease with a simple grin. It was magical, and, recalling those afternoons with him, she was struck by the remembrance that he always made the most of a situation. He always found something to make them laugh.

"I got you to smile. That's a step in the right direction," he said with satisfaction, but there was nothing smug about this. It was thoroughly disarming. "How fortunate I am that all isn't lost after all. I only wish to do what's right, you know, and I intend to see that you're repaid for last evening. If I could, I'd cross every palm in the realm to scotch the gossip, but I fear the events were of such a lurid and sensational nature that even my fortune doesn't wield sufficient power to stop the wagging tongues. Instead, I must take the lead, and from this moment onward everything I do in your regard will be above reproach. An announcement has been sent to *The Times*, the banns will be read this Sunday, and I intend that your betrothal and wedding festivities be the envy of every mama in Mayfair. We shall best the highest of the high sticklers at their own game."

Eleanor looked away from his intent blue-eyed regard. She had assumed that any wedding would be a hasty, secretive affair. Perhaps that was one reason why she rejected the notion. The prospect of marrying in a private ceremony as if it were something criminal was appalling to her. But Litchfield had no such intentions. Quite to the contrary—even Eglantine would approve of his plans. The most implausible picture of a fair knight astride a white charger flashed across her mind's eye. In a quite voice, she asked, "Why would you do all this?"

"Because it's what you deserve. Because a young lady only weds once and that day should rank among her fondest memories. It should exceed her dreams," Litchfield said, wishing that she would look up so he might discern whether or not his words caused her eyes to shimmer with golden highlights. He hoped that was the case, and in a low voice, he added, "Because this is the beginning of the rest of your life, and I'm going to guarantee that you never have anything less than the best."

His words managed to devastate the final vestiges of Eleanor's hostility, and she stared at him as if the breath had been taken from her lungs. To have received such lovely sentiments was beyond anything she had imagined. This was one of the most vivid moments of her life, and she would remember it always. The eyes that she raised to his were luminous, and she tried, but failed, to reply to him.

"Now go on and open your gift," he urged, knowing that his words had hit their mark.

Eleanor swallowed in an unaccountably dry throat and focused on the box. It was much better than having to meet his gaze or remain mute with nothing to say. She lifted the lid, folded back the top layer of tissue, and emitted a tiny gasp of wonder. Her heart somersaulted, and her fingers trembled as they touched the gold braid of a brand new pirate hat.

"I know it's not the usual sort of betrothal gift a gentleman gives a lady," he was saying, although she scarcely heard him over the pounding of her heart. "I trust you're not offended, but I was hoping that it might mean more to you than pearl ear bobs or a sapphire ring."

"I don't know what to say," Eleanor whispered, and when she looked up, her eyes blazed golden. He grinned at her, and she knew he had derived much pleasure from giving her this gift. In that instant, she thought of her father. He would never have acted like this, and Eleanor knew that any man who did something this considerate couldn't be like her father. More than anything Eleanor wanted to trust Litchfield, but she was afraid. Here, she had seen proof that he wasn't a total scoundrel, yet that fear would not allow her to dismiss her misgivings altogether. Fear, she found, was a powerful emotion. It was cold and paralyzing, and not a bit like the heat of anger which might have sparked her to leave before there was no turning back. She was more confused than ever with this topsy-turvy state of affairs, and she repeated, "I don't know what to say."

"A simple thank you would suffice."

"Yes, of course, but that's not what I meant. You're quite on the mark. The pirate hat means more to me than pearls or sapphires, but I can't accept a betrothal gift. It wouldn't be right when I don't intend—"

"Please don't say another word. I know the rest, and as far as I'm concerned the gift is yours whether or not we wed. And as for whether or not we're going to marry, I hope that hasn't yet been decided. You see, I was rather counting on your giving me a chance to prove myself."

Eleanor blushed. "I don't see anything wrong in agreeing to that."

"Thank you," Litchfield said with the most unfamiliar humility. He gave a short nervous cough, then continued, "I took the liberty of consulting with the Dowager Duchess of Exeter this morning."

Eleanor returned this revelation with an inquisitive stare.

"As I said, I only want what's best for you, and the intervention of a lady of her stature seemed prudent. Your abigail let it slip there was a connection, and I called upon her grace while you were resting."

"What did she say?"

"She asked us to tea. I believe she had some notions as to what's in your best interest. Will you talk to her? See what she has to say?" Litchfield held his breath waiting for her answer. Having already been to call upon the dowager duchess, he had been astonished at how easily her grace's favor had been secured in this delicate matter.

"Of course you're right, Litchfield," the lady had declared. "You should marry the gel, and I'll see to it she abandons those rackety notions of hers and accepts you." It was the dowager duchess who had reminded Litchfield to get an immediate announcement off to *The Times*, and she'd thoroughly surprised him when she pronounced that it wasn't in Lady Eleanor's best interests to remove her from his residence to reside at Exeter House until the wedding.

"Gel's reputation is already in a shambles, and if we want this to end in matrimony we most certainly don't wish to make it easy for her to avoid you. Proximity. That's what we must foster. I can trust you, Litchfield, if she stays under your roof, can't I?"

He'd replied in the affirmative, astonished and grateful and full of hope that no matter what happened when Mulgrave's daughter awoke this day it would turn out well in the long run. So far it was proceeding better than he could have imagined.

"Yes, my lord, I'll listen to her grace," Eleanor replied.

Well, it was going well with one exception, he thought with a rueful sort of expression. "I wish you wouldn't be so formal with me. You mustn't call me 'my lord.' "

"What should I call you?"

"Addison."

"But that's not proper." She was being stubborn. He recognized that in the way she tilted her chin.

"Ah, but when were we ever proper, Miss Carew?" He took a great risk and teased her in that wickedly beguiling tone of voice.

It was a good risk. The hint of a smile touched

her beautiful red lips, and golden highlights sparkled in her eyes. Even when she found it impossible to give him her trust, the effect he had upon her was magical. She was feeling light-headed and warm, and, oddest of all, he made her feel safe. Perhaps, she speculated, it wasn't the reaction that was incorrect—any woman might find Lord Litchfield hard to resist. Perhaps he *was* right, and it was her assumptions about him which were wrong. Perhaps, as he asserted, she only thought she knew who he was. Perhaps he was a man to trust, and therein lay her immediate future. She had promised to give him a chance to prove himself, and she must see it through.

"You must call me Addison as my friends and family do, and I should like to call you Nora, if you'd let me," he said, allowing himself to entertain the fantasy that very soon she would be his wife and he would hold her in his arms to whisper *Nora* against the creamy warm flesh of her throat.

"That was my mother's pet name for me," she said with sudden shyness. For a moment, it had seemed as if his clear blue eyes were caressing her, then it had passed.

"Ah, well, then I understand." The fantasy was doused. "If you'd rather I called you something else, I understand."

"No! That's not what I meant." Eleanor surprised herself with this quick denial, and in the silence that ensued, she lowered her eyelashes, then as swiftly she looked at him again. "Of course you may call me Nora. I—I believe I would like that. Truly."

"Then I thank you for the honor, Nora."

She rose and took his offered arm, and they were off to tea at Exeter House. How peculiar, Eleanor thought as Litchfield's town coach made the short trip to Exeter House, that it all seemed so simple and civil, so tidily wrapped up, when truth to tell she wasn't at all certain where it was going to end.

Thirteen

T EA AT EXETER House did not unfold the way
    Eleanor had anticipated. Of course, the Paul
de Lamerie silver service was the finest, and they
sat in the Blue Saloon overlooking the garden. Of
course, the dowager duchess received Eleanor as if
she were a dear relation. And of course, Eglantine
gloated most predictably over the miracle of romance which she had wrought. After all—her expression told anyone who cared to decipher
it—the match between Eleanor and Litchfield was
her doing. If it hadn't been for her insistence,
Eleanor would never have searched for the mysterious gentleman, and thus it was that Eglantine
couldn't wipe the silly grin from her face even
when her favorite jellied ham sandwiches and
powdered sugar cakes were served. She sat like
some overfed tabby cat, looking back and forth between Eleanor and Litchfield, occasionally inter-
rupting this study of the couple to nod her head in
satisfaction. Eleanor had expected no less.

As for the dowager duchess, her grace was as
unconventional as always, hardly batting an eye-
lash upon learning the details of Eleanor's humiliation at her father's hand. Nor did it faze her to
discover Eleanor had departed her father's town
house on Litchfield's arm, or that the two young

people were, in point of fact, already acquainted owing to the clandestine association in which they'd been engaged since sometime in May. Her grace gave a few disparaging clucks, a few censorious tuts, mumbled that Vile Villiers hadn't a redeemable bone in his body, and then thoroughly shocked Eleanor with a wholehearted endorsement of Litchfield's wedding plans.

It was at this point that the afternoon began to take a decided turn toward the unexpected.

"I knew Litchfield's family," the dowager duchess informed Eleanor while Eglantine was giving Litchfield a tour of the late duke's Roman statuary so that her grace might counsel Eleanor in private. "Litchfield's grandfather, the seventh earl, was master of the hounds in Hampshire. His father, too. Both excellent horsemen. And his mother. She was a lovely girl. Such a pity they won't be here for the wedding ceremony. Your mother, too. Lady Penelope. Such a pity. We shall miss them all, to be sure. But I shall be honored to stand in their stead and have already started thinking about your wedding fete, m'dear. It shall be here at Exeter House, of course, even though you shall remain at Litchfield's on Langham Place. I believe that's best, don't you agree?"

"To remain at Litchfield's?" Eleanor didn't like the idea. It didn't sound *best*, it sounded worst, and she stared at the dowager duchess with an expression of thorough astonishment. She would never have agreed to give Litchfield any sort of chance if she'd imagined she was going to continue sleeping beneath his roof, seeing him first thing every morning and last thing every night. The thought was most unsettling, not to mention highly improper. "I don't wish to disagree, your grace, nor to impose upon you, but I assumed I would be moving into Exeter House as soon as possible. This afternoon, once our tea was concluded."

"Move into Exeter House? Wouldn't be an imposition, but neither is it necessary. Whatever for, my dear? I don't mean to be cruel, but your reputation is quite in tatters already, and as you're soon to be Litchfield's countess this will be the surest way to begin learning one's obligations in such a large establishment." The dowager duchess sent up a silent prayer that the girl wouldn't challenge this explanation. It was a poor excuse, but the best she could devise on such short notice. To her satisfaction, Eleanor looked appropriately bewildered, and the dowager duchess plunged onward:

"Of course, you won't be in residence without a chaperon. I've a third cousin who lost her husband almost a year ago, but despite the passage of time she can't seem to escape her grief. I fear the colonel's demise was more than Lady Girouard could bear. They never had any children, you see, and Lady Girouard has been most dreadfully lonely these past months. No purpose, she laments. Cast adrift. Naturally, this would be the ideal solution for both of you. Lady Girouard shall move into Langham Place. She's an amiable sort, and I believe you'll find her more than tolerable."

"I see," mumbled Eleanor, not liking the perception that sometime since dawn the course of her life had been charted out for her. She knew the dowager duchess was well intended, even Litchfield gave that impression, but Eleanor couldn't help feeling as if she'd escaped her father's domination only to find herself being moved about like a pawn on a chessboard. Good manners, however, required that she keep such feelings to herself.

Despite her silence, Eleanor's reluctance was apparent to the dowager duchess, who tried another tack, casting Eleanor in the role of savior to the grief-stricken Lady Girouard. "And, of course, you shall be doing Lady Girouard an enormous service, m'dear. You've no notion how her spirits revived upon considering the importance of her mission. She's most eager to meet you. It shall do her a world of good to get out of that gloomy place of hers and be at your side."

Eleanor offered a politely crafted protest. "But even with Lady Girouard as chaperon do you believe Litchfield's home will be *safe*? It's his reputation that troubles me, your grace. Don't you fear for my virtue with a man of my father's ilk?"

"Not in the least, for you're quite mistaken, m'dear." The dowager duchess helped herself to a ham sandwich and set it on her plate with a sprig of watercress. "Your sire is a wastrel. Litchfield's merely a rogue."

"I'm not sure I see the difference."

"Well, you mustn't look to me for clarification. This is something you must discover for yourself, and in time, you shall."

"You speak in riddles, your grace."

"Mayhap." The dowager duchess enjoyed a bite of ham sandwich, then a sip of tea. She preferred black pekoe to which she added several cubes of sugar. "Tell me, Eleanor, have you ever wondered why Litchfield has been such an incorrigible scoundrel? Why it was he threw himself into the headlong pursuit of dissipation?"

"I supposed he liked it. My father always gave that impression."

The dowager duchess gave Eleanor an impatient rap upon her knuckles with the George II sugar tongs. "Just as I feared. You should be ashamed of yourself to judge a man without full knowledge of the facts. What do you know of him?"

"I know he gambles with unconscionable sums of money, drinks to excess, consorts with persons of low moral character, visits establishments of ill-repute, is not welcome in respectable drawing rooms and, according to Lady Soames, has vowed never to wed."

"Bah! And if I believed anything that dropped from Arabella Soames's lips we'd all be dancing with pigs in Smithfield Market. Besides that's not what I meant. Labels don't make a gentleman. Those things may be true enough, but they're of a transitory nature. Tell me, what do you know of Litchfield's family, his childhood, his life before they called him Fortune?"

"Very little," whispered Eleanor in soft reply as comprehension settled over her. He'd told her almost nothing about himself, and in retrospect she realized that was the way he'd wanted it. His control had been so clean, so practiced, that she hadn't seen how guarded he'd been with any word that might reference the past, how surgical he'd been with every hint of emotion.

"Well, if you're to marry the gentleman, it's time you got to know him."

"That's my intention, your grace, although not necessarily with an eye toward matrimony. I haven't actually accepted his proposal. I've only agreed to give him a chance to prove himself."

"Haven't accepted his proposal! How could you deny him? And don't even consider the trappings—the money, the title, the vast estates, or his charm and elegant good looks. How could you reject him when he feels the way he does? Don't you see how much he loves you?"

"You must be mistaken, your grace. I believe he cares in some way, but love? He has not spoken of it."

This elicited another rap with the sugar tongs. "And more the fool you are, young lady. Do you think a gentleman like Litchfield ever embarks upon anything he doesn't want? And could you imagine that such a man would ever marry for less than love? Believe me, I'm not mistaken. My Anthony was such a man. His grace vowed never to marry, yet here I am."

"I don't know what to believe, your grace," Eleanor said on a weary, dispirited sigh. She considered all the special touches in the pretty gold and plum bedchamber, and she recalled the expression upon his face when she had opened the betrothal gift. She thought of how he made her heart race, how he caused her legs to weaken when he kissed her and how he made her wish for more. Of Fate and dreams and a knight as fair as one of King Richard's own. And she thought of the whole great world she would never see. "I can hardly trust myself anymore," she confessed.

"Give it time," the dowager duchess replied with a comforting pat to Eleanor's forearm. The sugar tongs remained on the table. "You know, I see a bit of myself in you. Not a bit like Eglantine, either of us, the way she falls in and out of love, plunging headlong into this and that. Poor scapegrace gel never thinks, but she's a happy trusting soul. Never been confused. Mayhap that's our weakness. We think overmuch. Tell me, Eleanor, have you ever simply allowed yourself to feel, to act on instinct or make a decision without considering the repercussions? Which brings us round to a far more important question. How do you feel about Litchfield?"

"I liked him very much when he was Mr. Weare." That was an easy answer, and a smile actually turned up at the corners of Eleanor's mouth.

Her grace waved an impatient hand. It hovered over the sugar tongs. "That was then, m'dear. Let's focus on now and the future. Tell me, Eleanor, how did you *feel* when Litchfield told your father he would marry you?"

"I was furious. Horrified. Shocked." Her smile broadened, and delicate streaks of pale pink touched Eleanor's cheeks when she added, "And undeniably pleased that someone would take me away from there."

The dowager duchess laughed. "That's a good gel. Quite promising. I like that. And how do you feel when you're alone with him?"

The answer to this was not, however, something Eleanor could divulge to her grace, and pale pink turned to a startling scarlet flush that worked its way up her neck, across her cheeks, and all the way to her hairline.

Once again, her grace laughed. "I believe this is the greatest bit of fun I've had in a long time. And no, I'm not laughing at your expense, m'dear Eleanor. It's the memory of the follies of my own youth. History repeats itself, it seems, and I must confess to being thrilled at the chance to observe the twists and turns of romance when it's someone other than myself involved."

Eleanor regarded the dowager duchess as if the lady were a candidate for Bedlam.

"It'll all make sense soon enough, m'dear. Now let's ask the others to come back in. I'm sure Eglantine would enjoy some of those sugared cakes, and we must tell Litchfield about Lady Girouard."

Lord Fortune had never opened his mother's drawing room on Langham Place to Polite Society—he had shunned the *ton* and its requisite rituals—but now, with some four hundred invitations to the dowager duchess's ball to celebrate the wedding of the Earl of Litchfield to Lady Eleanor Villiers on mantels throughout the West End, it was evident that Litchfield intended to reclaim his place among the Upper Ten Thousand. The banns had been published for three consecutive Sundays at St. Pauls, the marriage seemed a certainty, and everything about Litchfield's behavior was above reproach. He had not returned to Lisle Street, had not even wagered in the book at White's. He spent mornings perusing the daily papers at his club or sparring in the ring at Gentleman Jackson's Boxing Saloon on Bond Street. Weather permitting, afternoons were reserved for tooling his curricle through Hyde Park in the company of Lady Eleanor and Lady Girouard, and in the evenings, he escorted the ladies about Town. Given his family standing and the endorsement of the Dowager Duchess of Exeter, even Almack's welcomed him, and Polite Society could do no less. Over the past three weeks a steady stream of callers had made their way to Litchfield's drawing room at Langham Place, and Eleanor's early afternoons were devoted to receiving these ladies and gentlemen.

"Is it getting any better?" Litchfield asked Eleanor as a serving girl entered the library with a tea tray. The daily pile of calling cards was remarkable, and he knew that acting as hostess to virtual strangers had at first been a strain on Eleanor.

"A little every day." Eleanor smiled, and when the serving girl had left she added two drops of brandy to his tea. He preferred it that way, and the brandy was their secret.

It had been raining since noon, a veritable downpour, and thus their carriage rode in Hyde Park was canceled. Lady Girouard had retired for a nap, and Eleanor and Litchfield had decided to share a late tea in the library. She was seated on the settee nearest the hooded fireplace from which a fire chased away the unseasonable chill. He relaxed in the upholstered Queen Anne armchair that had become his favorite seat. The comfortable piece of furniture was a new addition to the library, which was a different room these days.

Eleanor, who had been encouraged to explore the house at Langham Place, had been busy these past weeks. The watercolor of Litchfield's father rested on a gilt tabletop easel along with miniatures of Lady Penelope and an infant Eleanor; a riot of late spring flowers graced the marble pedestals on either side of the mantel; what remained of the collection of porcelain shepherdesses was displayed on a pretty inlaid table with turreted front corners; and there was the lingering scent of gentleman's lime cologne, for Litchfield found he preferred this room and liked to sit with Eleanor and hear what it was she had been doing and who she had received that day. Even when she was gone from the house, shopping with Lady Girouard or visiting the dowager duchess and Lady Eglantine, the library was where Litchfield spent his time when at Langham Place, which seemed to be more and more these days.

"Lady Girouard has been pleasant company?" Litchfield asked. Eleanor nodded yes, and he added, "Would you like her to stay after the wedding?"

"I would not like to turn her out," Eleanor replied, thinking that once again he seemed to be skirting any direct discussion of their future. It had been like this from the moment they had returned that afternoon from Exeter House. He might talk about Lady Girouard's future or of the merits of lemon wedding confections versus nutmeg and spice, but not about *them;* not about whether or not in getting to know him she had decided to remain with him. He was unfailingly polite, attentive, and generous, but he never, *never* brought up the subject of her feelings about their future. It troubled Eleanor. "You know, Addison, it seems prodigiously odd to me that while all of Mayfair expects us to be married in three days, this is the first you've mentioned it since the final reading of the banns a week ago Sunday."

"Ah, yes, well, it seemed things were proceeding favorably between us, and I didn't want to pressure you." He tried for a light tone, but this was serious. In the past weeks, his love for Nora had grown. Not once had he doubted his decision to marry her, but his faith that she would be his wife remained weak.

His comment made Eleanor think of how he managed to avoid revealing anything of himself. He talked about not pressuring her, but mentioned nothing of his feelings, and Eleanor couldn't resist asking:

"Are you saying that you would pressure me, if all was not proceeding according to plan?" Her eyes were golden bright.

"Are you teasing me, Nora?" Litchfield asked in that low voice that never failed to make her blush. He grinned, adoring the way her eyes sparkled and her lovely mouth turned up at the edges. He still thought about kissing those lips, of freeing Nora's Gypsy black hair to tumble about those creamy shoulders, but more than sensual fantasies he thought of sharing a lifetime with her. Stillness settled over his features, and he took a deep breath before saying, "Yes, the wedding is in three days, but you have never told me whether or not you'll stay with me." Another breath, a longer pause. His voice turned to a husky whisper. "Marry me, Nora, and I would give you your dreams."

Eleanor looked at Litchfield and saw expectation in his clear blue eyes. She saw the slight tension along his jaw, she'd heard his hesitancy, and she didn't doubt his sincerity. Still she asked, "What do you know of my dreams?"

Again, Litchfield grinned, for he'd come to know Eleanor quite well these past weeks. He'd anticipated this very question, and he knew the delicacy with which he'd have to handle his reply. "I know what you say, Nora. You say you'd like to be on your own, never to live at another's whim, that you'd like to make independent choices and see the world. But I don't think that's true," he ended very, very softly.

"What do you mean?" A tiny warning prickle of something like anxiety niggled at Eleanor. She wasn't angry at Litchfield. He never made her angry anymore. But she was surprised and a little frightened by what he'd said.

"I've watched you carefully these past weeks, Nora. You're different. The house is different. It's a home. As for you, I think you're happy here, and for those changes to have occurred, well, it seems so contrary to your dream that I couldn't help wondering why it was you ever yearned to be on your own in the first place."

The golden highlights in Eleanor's eyes flared, then dimmed. Sweet heaven, he knew the truth that she had been hiding deep inside, and she felt like a fraud. She didn't have to answer out loud. He knew why, and part of her resented Litchfield for knowing what it was that she'd been denying all this time. And another part of Eleanor melted at the thought that this man had cared enough to look into her soul with more consideration and honesty than she'd given herself. She had never been more vulnerable, not even sitting in her father's vestibule and being leered at by those men, and she bit her lower lip to prevent it from quivering, for she knew with a sudden and awful clarity that Litchfield had more power over her than her father had ever possessed.

"I think you were determined to find independence because you were afraid," he said with a tenderness that made Eleanor's heart skip a beat. She remained motionless, her heartbeat pounding in her ears, and although Eleanor didn't say a word the golden highlights in her eyes urged him to say more.

"I think you were afraid that if you depended on anyone—as your mother did—you might be left behind as she had been. And I think you feared being left behind because you truly desire everything your mother never had, everything that I might give you."

The teacup trembled in Eleanor's hand, and she set it down on its saucer with a clatter. She didn't know whether to laugh or cry. Litchfeld was right. All those dreams had been because she thought she couldn't have anything else. She'd been running away, and as she stared at Litchfield, Eleanor felt as if a great weight were being lifted from her shoulders. Of course, she wanted to see faraway places, but he'd seen the truth. More than faraway places she wanted a family and happiness and the security of knowing she could depend on one man, that she could trust someone with her dreams.

And she knew something else at that moment. She gazed at this man who wanted to give her her dreams, and Eleanor knew she wanted a future with Litchfield.

"Marry me, Nora, and I would give you your dreams," he repeated, as if he'd been reading her thoughts. "Think of all that I've given you in this short time. Imagine everything else I could give you. I could even make your dreams come true."

Eleanor wanted to cry. What he'd said was achingly beautiful, and she didn't doubt for one second that he meant every word of it, but it wasn't enough. The problem was he'd given her everything within his power, but he'd never given her something of himself. The fact that he had not shared himself with her was an omission that left a dark bruised spot upon Eleanor's heart. Litchfield was willing to give Eleanor her dreams, but he'd never mentioned his own. She still knew nothing about the past to which the dowager duchess had referred. Without that it was impossible for trust to blossom. And without trust, Eleanor couldn't truly love, for when she gave her heart it had to be without any reservation or lingering fears, it had to be with total trust.

"You're hesitating," he said with visible effort. There was a touch of panic in his voice. He'd been so certain of her, so sure of the future, their future. He hadn't expected her to hesitate now, not when he knew the truth and had offered Eleanor her heart's desire. "Why, Nora? What's wrong? You're not going to turn down my proposal, are you?"

"I accept your proposal, Addison," was her simple reply.

"But you don't sound like a besotted bride in the grips of true love," he said, fearing the future was slipping through his fingers. He'd done something wrong, but he didn't understand what it could be.

"I'm not," she whispered, sensing that this was going to wound him. He'd been nothing but kind and good and patient. She didn't want to hurt Litchfield, but it was the truth.

He felt as if the air had been punched from his lungs. "Why marry me then?"

"Because I know you'll take care of me. Because you're right. I have been happy here, and I think we can be happy together."

"And that's enough? That's all?" Litchfield was as provoked and as desperate as he sounded. "What more do you want, Nora? What more? A pound of flesh? All right, I love you. I've said it. Is that what you wanted?"

She flinched and lowered her lashes to conceal

her bitter disappointment. "Not like that. I don't want it. Not in frustration. Not touched with anger." She'd never felt such a distance between them than at that moment.

"What then? What's wrong?"

"You've showered me with material things, but nothing of yourself," she said with a quietness that revealed her own pain. She knew the dowager duchess had been correct. This man did love her, but it was a carefully guarded love that he'd only been able to reveal in anger.

"Nothing of myself! What's a declaration of love? It comes from me, from my heart, Nora. Isn't that enough? God knows I mean it, and I've never said those words to another woman, never felt this way before. Why do you think I never had my way with you? And why did I enter the game that night or even announce my intention to wed you? I could have done otherwise in all those situations. I was going to seduce you, y'know. I had every intention of doing just that and leaving you without a second thought, but I didn't. At first, I didn't understand what held me back. The truth was I'd fallen in love with you, Nora, that first afternoon in the rain." He gave a harsh laugh that had nothing of joy, but echoed instead with sorrow. He rose from the Queen Anne chair and stood before the settee to stare at her upturned face.

"You know, Nora, way back then I didn't understand what you wanted from me, and hell, it's no clearer to me now."

Without warning, he dropped onto one knee and took her hands in his.

"Please." She was very near to tears. "Don't do that. Please get up, Addison. We're to be married in three days. I've accepted your proposal, and I can truly say that I'm happy about that. I don't want to leave and go off on my own. I want to stay with you. I'm happy here. Happy with you. For now can't that be enough?"

"No, it's not enough," was Litchfield's rough reply. He stared at Eleanor, eye-to-eye, still on one knee. He drank in the sight of her courage and her beauty, the trembling in those moist red lips and the brush of high color across her cheeks. She was so perfect and so lovely, so near and yet so far. This could not be the end. "Devil take it, Nora. I've wanted you from the first moment I set eyes on you, and I still do. And I'll have all of you, do you hear? I'll have your heart and your mind, and I'll have you as my wife and in my bed because you love me. Not little pieces you're willing to parcel out."

He seized her elbows and pulled her off the settee and against his chest. Looking into her eyes, he drew a hard uneven breath before his hands framed her face and his mouth claimed hers with an unbearable almost violent hunger.

"Put your arms around me, Nora," he murmured against her lips.

Eleanor did as he asked, clinging to him, savoring the taste and feel of him, and responding to the yearning he aroused within her. She moaned and arched against him, her fingers threading through his thick hair.

Then he broke away. His expression was sober and sad as he pushed Eleanor to arm's length, then rose to his feet.

"There! Tell me, Nora, how does it feel to be trifled with?" And without waiting for her answer, Litchfield strode from the room.

Eleanor collapsed on the carpet, trembling with desire, the skirt of her muslin day dress spread out about her like a wilting flower. She could only stare through a mist of tears at the open library door where he had just left. She listened to the echo of his retreating footsteps as an awful hollow spot throbbed in the pit of her stomach, and she was filled with the horrible misgiving that marrying Litchfield was going to be the most stupendous mistake of her life.

Fourteen

LITCHFIELD COULDN'T SLEEP, not for the beastly
way he'd treated Eleanor in the library, not
for the way the rain thrashed at the windows, nor
for the way the relentless thunder seemed to taunt
him. There was no excuse for what he'd done, yet
he couldn't bring himself to apologize, not for the
burning shame he couldn't overcome. He'd been
ridiculously grateful that there were no engage-
ments on their social calendar for that evening. He
hadn't even joined Eleanor and Lady Girouard in
the dining room for dinner, offering instead a cow-
ardly excuse about overexerting himself at Gentleman Jackson's. He wanted nothing more than to
hide.

Closeted in the small study off his bedchamber,
Litchfield lounged on an overstuffed chair he'd
pulled near the window. His feet were propped on
the sill and the heavy brocade curtains had been
pulled back to reveal the storm. At first, he tried to
dull himself with a bottle of cognac, but instead of
forgetting what he'd done, the image of Eleanor's
face when he'd stopped kissing her to thrust her
away from him became more and more intense.
Her sleepy-lidded arousal would have been obvious to even a stranger, but there had been something else on her face that only he understood, and

it haunted him. A sort of panic, perhaps it had been regret, and Litchfield was tormented by the certainty of what that expression had meant.

He'd humiliated her. He'd used her. He'd subjected her to his whim, and he knew she had wanted to take back what she'd said about being happy and willing to marry him. He'd come to know her too well these past weeks not to be able to comprehend something that important.

Christ's nails, what had he done? It was almost as if he'd set out to ruin everything. Of course, that hadn't been his intention, and he wanted nothing more than to do whatever was necessary to make things right with Eleanor. But it went beyond an apology for his foul behavior this afternoon, and he still didn't know what it was that she wanted. The cognac left a bitter taste in his mouth, and he put the bottle down, then closed his eyes in an effort to forget himself in the sensations of the storm.

Someone knocked on the door. It was the maid, but he didn't let her in to light the wall sconces, and when the fire in the hearth had faded, the only light in the study came from the occasional flash of lightning. An hour or two passed. Litchfield dozed off to a troubled sleep dominated by thunder and violent silver streaks across a black skyline. His dreams were as ugly and disturbing as they had been sixteen years before when he hadn't been able to forgive himself for another failure.

Still asleep, he extended an arm and called out to someone. It was a harsh scream, piercing the dark night above a deafening crack of thunder, and with a sudden jerk he was awake. Beads of sweat dotted his brow, his breathing was agitated, and despite it all, Litchfield grinned.

* * *

The first thing Eleanor saw when she awoke was Litchfield sitting in a chair pulled close to the tented plum and gold bed. The violent storm of the previous night had passed, sunshine streamed into the Chinese bedchamber, and the pair of doves in the bamboo cage coed a soft morning lullaby.

"Good morning, Nora," he said. She was lovely even first thing in the day, and it tore at his heart that this might be the only time he ever saw her like this.

Eleanor blinked twice and pulled the counterpane about her neck. "How long have you been there?"

Litchfield gave a noncommittal shrug. "Did you sleep well?"

"Yes, thank you. I did," she replied with a qualm of disquietude, for it was obvious he hadn't passed a decent night. There were dark smudges beneath his eyes and tiny lines about his mouth that she'd never noticed before. His hair was tousled, there was a faint roughness along his jawline, and he wore the same clothes as yesterday. He looked a wreck. Still there was an unmistakable aura of contentment about him. There was a gentle smile on his lips that coaxed Eleanor to smile in return, and the light in his blue eyes was warm and tender, which caused Eleanor to feel weak and vulnerable. It didn't make sense. They had parted in anger, and all last night she had been distraught that he could have been so calculating. She had stood before the pier glass to practice the scathing set-down she had intended to deliver him, but now in the light of day her reaction to him was as confusing as it had always been. Instead of focusing on his intentional cruelty, she thought of how he'd held her in the boat after she'd almost been swept overboard and how he'd kissed her after she'd raced his curricle down the country lane.

The oddest notion flickered across her mind. It seemed she'd been in a deep slumber, rather like Cinderella waiting for someone to liberate her, and she wasn't sure what that meant.

"There's something I must tell you," he said urgently. He'd given this much consideration and knew what he had to say, but he worried that somehow she might stop him. He had to say it before that happened and there was no healing the damage he'd done.

"It must be very important." Her voice was still a whisper. The counterpane remained at her neckline.

Seeing her modesty, he hastened to explain, "I know I've no right to be here, but it couldn't wait."

"My curiosity is well piqued."

"Ah, yes, well," he mumbled that funny little trio of words he used when trying to discern the best way to begin something of importance. He inched forward on the chair, rested his forearms on the edge of the bed, and made himself meet her inquiring gaze. He wanted to take her hands in his as much for his own comfort as anything else; instead he forced his clenched fists to remain on top of the counterpane, and when he spoke, his voice was stilted and wooden.

"For so many years the only thing I've ever considered was my own immediate satisfaction. I'm sure that must have been obvious to you. I wasn't a man deserving of respect, or a man I would want courting my daughter. Then I met you, Nora, and something changed. I scarcely realized it at first, but it happened in such small increments that there was no way to fight it. Yesterday I told you that I love you, and because of that love I know it is your happiness—not my own—that I wish to see fulfilled. I shall set you free, Nora, and release you from our betrothal, if that's what it takes to make you happy. There was a sizable sum of money on the table that night at your father's. It's yours to do with as you wish."

"You speak as if I were nothing more than a possession to dispose of at will," she said sharply. How could he say that? she wondered with a surge of panic. Why didn't he understand that wasn't what she wanted anymore? She didn't want him to give her freedom, she wanted him to bring them closer, so close that nothing would ever make her doubt him again.

"A possession? No, Nora, that's the farthest thing from the truth." There was nothing stilted about his tone of voice any longer. It rang, instead, with tenderness.

"Lord Fortune's Prize," she challenged. "That's what the tabbies have been calling me behind their fans. Surely you had heard."

"And there's truth in that. Forgive me, Nora, for not confiding in you sooner, for you are much more to me. You are my heart's prize, and I shall always hold fiercely to the hope that one day I might claim your heart as you have claimed mine." He heard the ragged little catch in her breath, saw the tears swimming in her eyes, and he swallowed against what felt like a lump in his throat before he went on, "I know what it was you were talking about yesterday. You were right. I've never truly given anything of myself. Although I've been waiting, hoping and expecting you to trust me, *I* haven't trusted *you*. Actually, I haven't trusted myself, but that's a fine point when the truth is I haven't been open and honest with you."

Without further ado he handed her a flat leather box of the sort that might hold a necklace.

"What's this?"

"Something of myself," he said, and his eyes were full of trust and affection.

Eleanor opened the lid. There was a single shard of glass upon deep blue velvet. It was long and thin, rather like a raindrop, or a tear perhaps, and very sharp. She looked at him for an explanation.

"It wasn't true what I told you about the scar beneath my eye. Not a word of it. I lied, Nora. It wasn't a foolish tumble. It was a horrible tragedy that pierced my heart as surely as my cheek was cut." And then he told her about the fire and his father and trying to save his mother. He told her about his failure and his fear and the awful loneliness he couldn't deny since he'd met her.

"I love you," he concluded simply. "And I trust you, Nora. I trust you with my heart."

Eleanor's breath stopped altogether at the words she'd longed to hear. This was far sweeter than she had imagined, for she had not dared to dream this might come true. Slowly, she exhaled, then asked, "And can you ever forgive me for having such little faith in you?" She'd been willing to think the worst of him, rather than believe that he was a creature of frail human emotion hungering for wholeness.

"There is nothing to forgive."

"Yes, there is. I was stubborn and selfish and denied my true feelings. I denied love."

"Ah, Nora," he murmured on a husky moan of passion. "Are you saying you love me?"

"Yes, and I have for a very long time." She reached out one hand to caress the half-moon scar beneath his eye. "You were right. I did like Mr. Weare very much. I liked all those things he said and did and how he made me feel in my heart and mind and the pit of my stomach. I liked the way he finished my sentences for me and made my knees wobble. And I'm ready to trust you, Addison, with my dreams and my future. I'm ready to let you lead and guide me toward our future."

Nothing Eleanor could have said would have

pleased Litchfield more, and there was the passing
sensation of an unfamiliar moisture in his eyes as
he slid onto the tented bed to pull her into a tender embrace. The counterpane fell between them,
and tenderly, he placed his lips over hers. The heat
from his body warmed her, his hands winding
through her thick black hair were powerful and
compelling, and she surrendered to the magic of
his kiss.

"I believe this is supposed to happen on our
wedding night," she teased in that saucy voice he
had missed these past weeks. Their breaths mingled. "This is most unseemly, sir."

His mouth moved lower to caress the pulse in
her throat. That slender neck, those lovely shoulders were as creamy as he had imagined, and his
teeth stole gentle tastes of her. "Do you care?" he
groaned on a husky underbreath.

She ran her hands across his back, reveled in the
hardness of the taut muscles beneath his shirt, and
her answer was lost as she surrendered to him, savoring the intimacy of his touch and giving in to
her boundless love.

L'ENVOI

February's End

"ARE YOU SORRY we're back in England?" Litchfield asked Eleanor as the heavy coach in which they were riding rocked over a winter-rutted road. His words, a low tentative whisper, fell upon her cheek where she rested her face against his shoulder. Traveling was tiring, and they had been on the road since mid-afternoon when their ship had docked at Portsmouth. The sun had set and crude curtains were fastened across the carriage windows, but still the crisp night air seeped inside the vehicle. It was cold and damp, and from outside, there was the pungent scent of peat fires that he found so peculiarly English. They'd been away for a long time and Litchfield was glad to be back, but he wasn't sure about Eleanor. Anxiously, he waited his wife's reply.

Eleanor didn't answer right away. Instead she reached out for Litchfield's hand, tilted her head to one side and smiled up at him. He'd given her her dreams, and she couldn't ask for more. In Paris, they had been received by Louis XVIII, attended the opera, visited Versailles and strolled in the Bois de Bologne, and after that, it had been on

180

to Rome, Venice, Florence, Vienna, Budapest, Athens, and Constantinople. For seven months they had followed the changing seasons, kept away from the crowds and vestiges of Napoleon's army, and they had seen the wonders of the world. Eleanor had climbed to the top of the Acropolis, sailed the Bosporus, walked among the nomadic tribes of Palestine, and at Giza, Litchfield had arranged for her to ride a camel across the ocean of sand. And everywhere she acquired mementos of their travels. Paintings and statuary, exotic furnishings, porcelains, colorful carpets, and yard upon yard of fabulous silks. They were treasures for Litchfield Park; Eleanor intended, in turn, to bring her husband's dreams to reality.

There was something he wanted as much as she had wanted to see the world, something that had been very important to him for many years, and she'd sensed it ever since he'd taken her to Litchfield Park that afternoon in August. It had been two days after their wedding in St. Paul's, and only a brief stop on their way to the boat that would ferry them across the Channel, but it was a stop he'd had to make before he left England, a stop that had revealed so much to Eleanor.

She hadn't been prepared for the ruins; he had never discussed the actual devastation. Nor had she been prepared for the change this sight wrought on Litchfield when he walked her through the tangle of untended rose bushes that had once been his mother's garden. She'd never known Litchfield to be as quiet and withdrawn as he was when he stood and stared at the blackened timbers of the once-great house.

"You'd never know it, but this was once the happiest place I could imagine," he'd said in a voice that seemed to come from very far away, and her heart had ached for him. The sun had been bright that afternoon and he'd shielded his eyes, hiding his expression, but she'd still seen how his cheek muscles tensed before he'd continued, "I used to play this game with my mother. It's almost too silly to talk about . . . but never having children other than myself, my mother dreamed of grandchildren, and we played this game—you mustn't laugh—naming all my sons and daughters and describing their antics. Of course, I was only ten or eleven and could scarcely relate to the notion of being a parent, so Robert and Andrew, Cecily and Bess were my brothers and sisters. And this was where they played hoops and tag and all variety of imaginary games with pirates and knights and fierce dragons."

Eleanor had been at a loss for words. She'd found herself precipitously close to tears and had remained silent as he'd walked round the ruin. Rooks had taken up residence in the crumbling chimneys, their cries had echoed across the untended lawns, and as Eleanor watched Litchfield she'd begun to see the truth. This visit was not about saying farewell, it was about searching and hoping for a new beginning, and she went after him to walk by his side.

"You'd like to rebuild," she had said very softly.

"If the time was right."

"Is now that time?"

"No, first I must give you some of your dreams. I intend to show you faraway places," he'd said without any trace of pain or regret.

And so they had left England and Litchfield Park behind, but Eleanor hadn't forgotten that afternoon in the overgrown rose garden, and while they were in Italy she'd consulted with the respected architect Marcus Virgili and commenced a plan of her own.

"Am I sorry to be back in England?" Eleanor repeated Litchfield's question, her thoughts no longer focused on the past, but on the moment at hand and the future. "I would never be sorry, Addison, as long as we were together. How could you ask such a thing? We're going home."

Her answer pleased him, and his lips touched the top of her head. The sweet scent of lavender was as familiar as it was comforting, and his chest swelled with emotion. He hoped he hadn't made the wrong choice. He wanted nothing but the best for Eleanor, but he wanted this too. "It won't be much of a home at first, you understand. At least not for the next several months. Although the caretaker's cottage is comfortable, I promise."

"I'm sure I'll survive." Eleanor's smile broadened with the joy of her secret, and if there had been sufficient light in the carriage Litchfield would have seen the explosion of golden highlights in her eyes.

The carriage had reached the turnoff, and the driver slowed the pace since the driveway was in worse condition than the public road. As a boy Litchfield had always ducked his head out of the carriage window to watch and wait for his first sight of the rooftop. Instinct propelled him, and he did the same now, silently cursing his foolishness, but instead of heartache, his spirits soared. He could hardly believe it when the carriage rounded the final bend, and there against the night sky was the majestic silhouette of a rambling manor house with pitched rooftops and chimney pots saluting the stars.

"What is this, Nora?" he asked when he finally found his voice. "What have you done?"

She laughed, sweet and light, a lyrical note of pleasure, satisfaction and love. "Why do you think I had such a lot of correspondence? Did you never wonder what I was doing? Or why I was so busy collecting and shipping wherever we went? I decided the statuary of the children we saw in that village in Lydia would be splendid in the rose garden, and of course, there is a gallery for all those paintings you admired. Lots of light in the gallery and throughout the house, Senori Virgili assured me. Very modern, you know, and rows of windows facing out on the garden. We'll be able to watch the children play."

The carriage came to a stop, and Litchfield gazed at the house in wonderment as an image of the dark past rose before his mind's eye and with it a fleeting instant of fear at the memory of what loneliness had meant. Then it was gone as the moon peeped out from behind clouds to cast its silver light on Litchfield Park. Thousands of tiny windowpanes sparkled like the endless stars of the universe, and Litchfield saw nothing but the brightness of a future filled with infinite possibilities.

Eleanor held her breath, fearing that she should not have done so much on her own. She had never stopped to think that this wasn't the right thing. He had given her so much and all she had wanted was to do the same in return. She had wanted to give him his dreams.

"It's not quite done yet, and the last of the furnishings have yet to arrive. I believe a few of the carpets are still to be put down," she said in a small voice. "But Senori Virgili wrote in his last letter that it's quite livable—"

"Oh, Nora, it's splendid. Magnificent. You're magnificent, and I love you, Nora." He reached out to caress her face, devouring her with his gaze, and his voice fell to a husky underbreath. "I love you so much that sometimes it hurts."

She blushed, for she'd come to know what exquisite pleasure lay behind that suggestive velvety tenor in his voice and what it was he was thinking when he focused so intently upon her lips. "I know." She turned her face to kiss the palm of his hand. "It's the same for me."

From outside there was a rumble of approaching thunder.

"Oh, no, not rain," Eleanor murmured. "I wanted to show you the rose garden."

"What's a bit of rain to us? Besides, we've a lifetime ahead for rose gardens. Right now I'd rather you showed me inside." Litchfield flung wide the carriage door to leap down. He offered Eleanor a hand to alight, and, arm in arm, they made their way toward the front door which was open and through which welcoming light streamed down the granite steps beckoning them to enter. At the threshold, Litchfield stopped.

"Is something wrong?" Eleanor inquired.

"Only if you object to a husband kissing his beautiful wife," he murmured as his mouth claimed hers, and, while his kiss deepened, he swept Eleanor off her feet to carry her over the threshold and into their home where love and laughter and dreams would always have a life of their own.